ALSO BY KAY L. MOODY

Fae and Crystal Thorns
Flame & Crystal Thorns
Shadow & Crystal Thorns
Blade & Crystal Thorns
Curse & Crystal Thorns
Wrath & Crystal Thorns
Standalone: Nutcracker of Crystalfall

The Fae of Bitter Thorn
Heir of Bitter Thorn
Court of Bitter Thorn
Castle of Bitter Thorn
Crown of Bitter Thorn
Queen of Bitter Thorn

The Elements of Kamdaria
The Elements of the Crown
The Elements of the Gate
The Elements of the Storm

Truth Seer Trilogy
Truth Seer
Healer
Truth Changer

Visit **kaylmoody.com/beauty** to download a bonus
story, *Bargain of Power and Beauty*, for free.

KAY L. MOODY

NUTCRACKER
OF CRYSTALFALL

A FAE AND CRYSTAL THORNS NOVELLA

Nutcracker of Crystalfall
Fae and Crystal Thorns series, standalone
By Kay L. Moody

Published by Marten Press
3731 W 10400 S Ste 102, #205
South Jordan, UT 84009

www.MartenPress.com

Cover by Angel Leya
Edited by Sara Lawson

ISBN: 978-1-954335-12-7

CRYSTALFALL
Amberglow Marshes
Gilded Labyrinth
Mushroom Patch
Emerald Lake
Diamond Isles
Gemfields
Celestine Meadow
Forest of the Wraiths
Crystalfall Castle
Goldvein Mountains
Rubyrise Mountains
Lifespark Tree
Pixie Grove
Mortals Land
Valley of Beryl
Sapphire Falls
Crystals Caves

1

TODAY WAS THE LAST DAY of Clara's life. Though she'd technically still be alive tomorrow, everything she'd ever loved would be ripped away from her. The few bright spots in her gloomy, seventeen and a half years of life would be snuffed out and replaced with even darker, gloomier things. She had one last day to enjoy herself. One last day before everything changed.

But how could she enjoy herself with such a future looming ahead?

Her fingers twitched over the teacup in her hands. Doing her best to forget the event that would take place the next day, she used a dark cloth to polish the outer surface of the porcelain.

After conspiring with her estate's baker, she had managed to paint and bake a protective glaze over the cup and saucer that would protect the designs she had spent months creating.

The polishing cloth now helped to make its surface shine. Delicate purple flowers and green leaves stood out against the bright white background of the small cup. She'd even strategically painted lines of gold around the teacup's edge and handle to give it a luxurious feel. Clara's lady's maid, Heidi, would feel like a noble herself whenever she used the cup and saucer.

That thought brought a little smile to Clara's lips. Maybe her lady's maid wasn't allowed to stay with Clara after tomorrow, but at least she'd be able to leave Heidi a gift she'd never forget.

With the polishing finished, Clara's thumb traced a bundle of the purple flowers she had painted. This particular bundle held a secret only Heidi would recognize. The flowers along the outer edge of the bundle were slightly darker, which created the shape of a ring. Others wouldn't notice the ring shape easily, but even if they did, they wouldn't understand the significance.

Only Heidi would know the ring shape was meant to commemorate a brass ring Heidi had received from her mother as a child and, sadly, had lost recently. But the painted flower ring on the teacup in Clara's lap was the exact same size and shape as that lost ring. Of course, it would never be the same as the real ring, but at least it gave Heidi a way to remember the special item.

Boisterous laughter rang out near Clara as a young couple floated past her with nearly empty glasses of wine in their hands. They wore silk party clothes, and the woman had her white-blonde hair expertly braided into a bun with soft curls, bright red flowers, and small fruits decorating it further. Judging by the direction the couple walked, they were on their way to refill their glasses.

Nearly all the guests had arrived. If some of them were already on their way to get a second glass of wine, she needed to hurry and place her gift for Heidi under the Christmas tree. Using the brown paper she had nicked from the kitchen, Clara carefully wrapped the teacup and saucer and positioned them inside a small brown box.

Spools of silk ribbon covered the table at her side. She chose a pretty blue ribbon with embroidered purple swirls. After unspooling it a bit, she eyeballed the length and then cut it. Her lips pursed as she examined it. The length would be perfect for Heidi to use as a hair ribbon.

No one else would ever think to use a gift wrap ribbon in their hair. No one else would ever imagine the length would be perfect for such a thing. But Heidi always appreciated Clara's talent for perfectly estimating the size and shape of things. Her lady's maid would know without even asking that Clara had cut it that length on purpose.

With the gift finally wrapped, Clara held it gently in both hands and started across the room. The dark walnut hardwood floor creaked under her feet, but with the violins and cello playing nearby, she could barely hear it.

Her gaze drifted to the Christmas tree in the center of the room. Its evergreen branches stretched so high, the tip nearly reached the chandelier hanging from the ceiling. A massive circular blanket sat at the base of the tree, catching the wax from the candles above. White candles adorned the needled branches, their little lights flickering with the same delight that filled the rest of the room. The wrapped presents sitting under the tree already piled high.

Dozens of guests crowded the normally-empty spaces of the large room. They ate and drank, danced and laughed. An almost-smile played at her lips at the sight of them. The guests were always her favorite part of her parents' annual Christmas party. With so many people watching, her parents had always been forced to get her fine and fancy gifts. Otherwise, their neighbors might guess how cruel her parents really were.

It did not fill her with joy to know she now needed assistance from one of them. Her pink silk skirts swished as she ambled through the room. It only took a moment to spot her mother. The woman's soft brown and gray hair had been braided with ribbon that matched her yellow and red dress. Her voice reverberated through at least one third of the room as she laughed and gossiped with her favorite women in their town.

Judging by the splashes of wine on her hand, she was already past her second glass and well into her third. Better to avoid Mother then. After that much wine, she was more likely to expose Clara's secret by accident—a secret no one except her father, mother, Heidi, and a few tutors knew.

Clara's shoulders tensed as she changed direction, heading toward the plushy chairs in front of the large fireplace at one edge of the room. At least her father sat alone as he leaned over the short wooden table in front of him, probably finishing a few last pieces of the paperwork that would spell out Clara's doom.

She darted toward him, grateful to have found him alone. Coming to his side, she knelt on the rug at his feet and held the gift and a small tag out to him.

After glancing over one shoulder, she leaned in close to whisper. "Could you address this for me?"

He had completely ignored her until that moment. As soon as the words left her lips, his gaze shot upward to scan the area around them. He found them in complete privacy, just as she had observed a moment ago. That didn't stop him from snatching the tag from her hand with a glare.

"What shall I write?" His gruff voice sounded even more gravelly than usual. His recent cough probably attributed to it, but the sound still made her limbs shake.

She gulped. "From Clara."

He rolled his eyes, clearly expecting her to say who the gift was *for* before she said who it was *from*. But she knew better than to give that away yet.

Despite his eye rolling, he did write the words in his sweeping, beautifully curved handwriting. More than anyone, he didn't want her secret getting out. So, he'd help begrudgingly as long as it didn't look suspicious. "What else?" Even in a whisper, he managed to make the words feel like an ugly shout.

"To," she continued, purposefully waiting until he started writing before she said more. When his pen stopped, she took a deep breath. "Heidi."

The snarl she expected bloomed across his face even fiercer than she had imagined. He bared his teeth as he leaned closer to her. "You have only one gift to give, and it's for a *servant*?"

Clara leaned back as she lifted her palms in a posture of surrender. "Heidi already helped me address my other gifts. We did it days ago."

He continued to snarl with his nose now twitching as he scrawled the name onto the tag. It looked far less beautiful than his previous handwriting. At least he had written it.

Just as she reached to pluck the tag from the table, an icy gust of wind shot across the room. Father had to grip the tag a little tighter to be certain it didn't blow away.

Both of them glanced toward the heavy wooden doors that had just been opened to the world outside. Five people entered the room, all dressed in fine silks and fur coats. Lord Metternich and his wife's eyes twinkled when they caught sight of the decorated Christmas tree. Their oldest son, Hans, and his wife smiled at the room as they shrugged their coats off.

And then there was Fritz, the person who would soon end her life as she knew it. Clara shuddered at the sight of him. The young man was a few years older than her. He wore what seemed to be a permanent scowl that even darkened his blue eyes. His golden-colored hair shifted lazily over his head as he scanned the room. When a servant helped remove his coat, he immediately adopted a threatening stance and glare, causing the servant to cower. Whatever words he had just spoken could not have been pleasant.

Upon seeing Fritz, Clara's stomach curled into a tight knot. Her throat ached when she tried to swallow. She knew it was useless, but she turned to her father anyway. Maybe one last appeal would work. Maybe she could change his mind if he heard the ache in her voice.

"Papa, please don't make me marry him."

Her father's eyes flashed as he glanced around to make sure no one had overheard. Once satisfied they were still speaking in private, he looked down his nose at her. "Whyever not?"

After kneeling at the side of his chair for so long, her knees had started to cramp. She swallowed hard. "He's horrid."

Her father's eyebrows pinched together until a crease formed between them. "A horrid man for a horrid girl." Now, he raised one of his eyebrows. "It seems you two are a perfect match."

The words alone were enough to tighten the ache in her throat even more, but then he crushed the tag in his hand. With a flick of his wrist, he tossed the crumpled paper into the roaring fire at his side.

"Get that gift out of here. I won't have a servant's present under the tree with all the other gifts." He dipped his head toward the ribboned box on the table, but at the last moment, he also swept his hand across the table to knock the box off it.

Sucking in a gasp, Clara barely caught the small gift before it fell. With the table so low to the ground, the teacup and saucer probably wouldn't have broken, but she didn't want to take that chance. She had spent months painting the porcelain. And it was meant for the only true friend she had.

Pulling the box tight against her stomach, Clara stood to her feet and nodded a quick goodbye to her father. It seemed she would have to get her mother to address the tag, after all.

Just as her silk skirts started swishing, her gaze snagged on Fritz. He shoved a servant out his way so he could reach the platters of food on a table faster.

A chill slithered down her spine. Maybe she needed Mother, but she wasn't about to go near her now. Not with Fritz nearby.

She'd do anything to avoid her betrothed for as long as she possibly could. Knowing him, he'd probably find a way to terrorize her sooner rather than later. She'd just try to keep to the edges of the room until then.

2

Since the main food tables were off-limits for Clara right now, she headed over to a narrow table covered with bowls of hazelnuts, macadamias, and chestnuts. Reaching for the nearest nutcracker, she placed a macadamia nut inside its mouth and lowered the lever.

Instead of hearing a nice crack, the shell stayed completely intact. Her mouth screwed into a knot as she set the nutcracker aside and reached for another one. The second one didn't crack her nut as much as smash it, so she had to pick out pieces of shell from the squashed nut before she could enjoy it.

While carefully plucking out broken pieces, she vaguely noticed someone join her at the table. Without even choosing a nutcracker, a sharp crack soon sounded. Her fingers still held her smashed nut from which she had nearly removed all the shell pieces, but her gaze trailed over to the nearby hands now reaching for a second nut.

The man plucked a hazelnut from a bowl and held it tightly between his finger and thumb. Another moment later, the nutshell split apart as easily as if it had been an eggshell. She almost didn't believe it, except he picked up a macadamia nut and cracked open the shell with his bare hands exactly like he had a moment ago.

Clara's eyes opened wide. "How did you do that?" The words came out in a rush as she glanced up to see who had done such an incredible thing.

But as soon as her gaze met the young man's face, her head immediately dropped. She lowered her chin to her chest and took a small step back.

"What is it?" the man asked after seeing her reaction. He patted his overcoat. "Do I look strange to you?"

Involuntarily, her gaze lifted to his once again. Now that he mentioned it, he *did* look strange. No, strange wasn't the right word. He looked wondrous. Magical. She had never seen anyone with such exquisite features, especially not someone only a few years older than her.

Sharp cheekbones perfectly accented his stormy gray eyes. He had fair skin and a crop of brown hair that looked shinier than her pink silk dress. His broad shoulders and strong arms gave the impression that he could probably lift her off the ground as easily as he had cracked those nuts. Easier maybe.

"Why did you look away from me like that?" He patted his blue scarf and blue overcoat that almost looked like a soldier's uniform. Except no soldiers in her town ever wore blue, especially not light blue brocade with swirling silver designs. She didn't know of any nearby countries whose soldiers had such uniforms.

She raised a hand to wave away his worry. "It's not the way you look, it's just…" She swallowed and lowered her chin again. "We haven't been formally introduced."

Out of the corner of her eye, she could just make out his lowered eyebrows. He didn't look confused; he looked aghast. After a small shake of his head, he cleared the expression away to reveal one of politeness. "Formally introduced. Right. I am Revyn."

It might have offended her that he didn't extend a hand toward her to shake in greeting, except she was too surprised by his name to even notice.

"Revyn? I have never heard such an unusual name. Is that your house name or your personal name?"

He mouthed the words *house name* and then shook his head. That same polite expression returned. "Revyn is my personal name. I believe as part of the formalities, you should state your name as well, correct?"

Nothing about this conversation followed the typical way people were formally introduced. That usually happened with a mutual acquaintance making the introductions. But this young man had probably just had one too many glasses of wine. What did it really matter anyway? This was a Christmas party. Her life was about to change, and not for the better, so what did she care about formalities?

She held out one hand toward him. "I'm Clara from the House of Reginar." She gestured vaguely at the room. "*This* house. My father is Lord Reginar, which leads me to ask, how do you know my father?"

"Know him?" The young man's head tilted to the side as he narrowed one eye. He gave off the distinct impression that he was trying to figure out not the answer to her question but why she had even asked it.

He also glanced down three different times at her hand, which was still extended toward him, but didn't seem to know what she expected him to do with it.

Once she lowered her hand back to her side, he finally seemed able to speak again. He ran a hand through his silky hair and flashed a roguish smile. "What was it you asked me earlier? You wanted to know how I did something, I believe."

The words disarmed her completely. Her cheeks suddenly tingled with heat as an involuntary smile crept through her lips. She placed a hand on her collarbone and had the sudden urge to fan herself. "Uh, it was…" She bit her bottom lip. "Oh, I wanted to know how you cracked those nuts with your bare hands."

His eyebrows twisted in confusion as he plucked a nut from the nearest bowl. Without showing the slightest strain in his face, he pinched the nut until the nutshell perfectly cracked in half. "Like that?"

Her eyes widened at the sight while the heat in her cheeks burned even hotter. If she dared to speak, her words would surely come out breathless.

Revyn gestured toward a bowl. "How do *you* crack them?"

Grateful for a chance to break her gaze away from him, she grabbed a hazelnut and stuffed it into a nutcracker's mouth. After lowering the lever as quickly as possible, it still only caused a small fracture across the shell's surface. She wrinkled her nose at the pathetic outcome.

Shrugging, Revyn reached over and cracked the nut for her. Then he took a few more from the bowls, cracked them, and set them in front of her too.

"Thank you," she said as she stuffed a macadamia into her mouth.

He blinked in astonishment. After glancing around the room, he turned back to her with a dark expression. "You should not say those words to me."

Before she could react to the strange response, his blue knit scarf was caught in a gust of wind from the front door and flew off his neck. He darted after it and soon got lost in the crowd.

Warmth still prickled in her cheeks as she tossed a hazelnut into her mouth. She'd probably never see him again, but she still marveled at the meeting. How strangely remarkable to meet a nutcracker…man.

Her mind was so thoroughly engrossed in the memory of Revyn that she hardly noticed she had eaten the nuts he'd cracked for her. And she definitely wasn't thinking straight when she meandered over to the food tables to gather a plate for herself.

With her gift to Heidi under one arm, Clara piled carrots drizzled with a honey and balsamic glaze onto her plate. Then she added a slice of wild duck with orange sauce and finished by grabbing a plump sausage. She managed to gobble down half the sausage before running into trouble, but soon she was reminded why she'd been avoiding the food tables.

Her nonchalant walk ended with a start when she found Fritz in a corner of the room watching a few young ladies dance. Although, he wasn't even watching them. He was leering at them a little too gratuitously for someone who was currently engaged to another woman.

She tried to back away without him noticing, but he glanced up as soon as she attempted it, sneering at her.

Since she couldn't avoid him, she sneered right back. "You probably shouldn't stare so salaciously at other young women when you and I are getting married tomorrow."

His hand shot forward. For a moment, she thought he might be reaching for her body, but he grabbed the gift box she was holding instead. "Thinking of the wedding, huh? This must be for me then."

He ignored her protests as he tore off the bow, lifted the lid, and carelessly threw off the brown paper protecting the porcelain. He laughed when he saw the items. "Did you paint this? How quaint."

"Give that back," she said through her teeth, which he completely ignored.

"I suppose no one told you, but I do not care for purple flowers." Holding her gaze steadily, he gripped two opposite sides of the teacup and yanked. Before she could reach out, he'd broken the teacup in half.

She gasped.

"I suppose now there's no use for this either." He threw the saucer onto the hardwood floor where it promptly split into three different pieces.

Tears pricked her eyes as her hand flew to cover her open mouth. "How could you?"

A vicious grin lifted his mouth. "You must have really cared about those pieces if they were enough to make you cry."

She had spent months of painstaking work designing and painting the cup and saucer. Maybe she didn't have the skill of the most famous artists, but her flowers were certainly beautiful. And now, all of her hard work had been destroyed. Her one last gift to the only person who had ever treated her with dignity was broken and lay in pieces on the ground.

Fritz laughed and ground the fragments into the floor with the heel of his boot until they shattered even more. He then dropped the cup pieces on top.

Uneven tears slipped down her cheeks. She tried to control her breathing, which had turned unnaturally quick.

Suddenly, Fritz leaned closer and whispered. "Everyone says there's something wrong with you. Something your parents keep secret."

A breath shuddered through her, and she immediately tried to gulp it down. It wasn't as if she had an extra limb or accidentally killed people in her sleep. It was that she couldn't read or write no matter how many tutors had tried to teach her throughout the years.

It wasn't her fault letters jumped around and rotated whenever she tried to look at them. When she concentrated very, very hard, she could read a little, but never out loud. And even then, it took so long to decipher each letter that comprehension became nearly impossible. One of her tutors had the same condition, but even that tutor had given up. Apparently, Clara's condition was much worse, and so, she was written off as a lost cause.

She could enjoy the beauty of handwriting, and she had no trouble reproducing actual objects like flowers, but letters and numbers liked to dance so much she couldn't dream of reading and writing the way others did. Still, it wasn't like she was a demon or a criminal.

Even now, she didn't understand why her parents were so mortified by her condition that they had kept it secret all these years.

A wild flash lit up Fritz's eyes. "Whatever your secret is, I don't care. I want to make it clear, I have no desire for you at all. I can easily find *companions*," he glanced pointedly at the nearest young ladies, "to satisfy my needs. From you, I only need one thing, and that is your money."

One last tear trailed down her cheek as she lifted her chin in the air. Maybe her hands still trembled from the emotion inside her, but she could control it well enough to speak. "I should have known a second-born child like you would feel that way. You've spent your whole life trying to measure up to your brother, Hans. Maybe you've learned ambition, but you know nothing of honor or decency."

"Decency." He laughed and used his boot to smash her teacup even more. "Once we're married, your father will make me rich. Then I'll finally emerge from my brother's shadows. I'll be the richer brother. The *better* brother. Just like I've always deserved."

With one last crush of his heel, he stomped off into the crowd. The moment he neared the young ladies he'd been admiring, they immediately backed away, as if he carried with him a stench they couldn't bear.

He ground his teeth at their reaction, curling one hand into a fist at the same time. His feet struck the ground harder with each step. When he noticed one of the young ladies happily talking to a different young man, Fritz stole the man's scarf straight from his neck.

The scarf's blue knit design made it easy to recognize. It was Revyn's scarf. The nutcracker man whirled around to find his missing accessory.

Fritz pulled it away just fast enough that Revyn couldn't grab it. Then—with Revyn watching—Fritz snatched a knife from a nearby table and slashed a cut straight through the center of the scarf.

As charming as he had been while cracking nuts, Revyn's face now looked murderous. And while Clara thought Fritz might have deserved injury for his actions, the strange young man probably wouldn't like the consequences such an action would bring.

Determined to halt a confrontation between them, she marched forward. Hopefully she could calm things down before someone lost an eye…or an arm.

3

, Clara mentally prepared to throw herself between the two irate young men. By the time reached them, her heart twisted with more hysteria than she could have imagined.

The strange nutcracker man, Revyn, glared right past her and over to Fritz. Revyn's nose flared with each of his heavy breaths. Across from him, Fritz looked just as ready to tear Clara apart as he was to tear apart Revyn.

More people gathered nearer at every second, so she only had a few seconds before this turned into something truly terrifying. Taking a step toward her betrothed, she grabbed him by the arm and squeezed.

Luckily, her voice came out low enough that no one else could hear, except possibly Revyn.

"Calm yourself, Fritz." She raised an eyebrow. "You wouldn't want to do something to make my father change his mind about tomorrow, would you?"

His face reddened as he ripped his hand away. She sent another pointed stare straight into his eyes, but then her words seemed to sink in. He bared his teeth and took a small step back. He glanced at Revyn again, this time seeing his broad shoulders and carefully kept uniform.

With a loud huff, Fritz turned on his heel and vaguely gestured toward the young man he'd just been glaring at. "You aren't worth my time anyway."

As he stomped off, Clara found both of Fritz's parents staring at him with arms folded across their chests. His mother shook her head, which went perfectly well with the deep frown Fritz's father directed toward his son. Fritz just scowled at them and continued stomping across the room.

Though Fritz's brother, Hans, sat at a nearby table, he seemed completely oblivious to the whole ordeal. He sat in a cushy chair with his wife on his lap. They both snickered as he fed her grapes.

Seeing him must have irritated Fritz further. He had very nearly punched a man, even stolen the attention of more than half the room, and yet, his perfect brother who could do no wrong hadn't even noticed.

After seeing Hans, Clara glanced back at Fritz's retreating form. His shoulders slumped even lower than before.

She didn't bother looking to see if her own parents had noticed anything. They stopped paying attention to her years ago. Despite her threat to Fritz, nothing could stop their wedding now. Unless, perhaps, she somehow managed to run away. But even if she did get away, she had nowhere to go.

Her gaze slid back over to the other young man involved. Every trace of anger had been wiped from Revyn's face. Now he stared with genuine horror at the slashed blue scarf in his hands. Maybe it was just the flickering candlelight, but his fingers seemed to shake a little.

Placing a hand behind one of his elbows, Clara led him to the darkened corner of the room where she'd wrapped Heidi's gift. It didn't take much prodding to get Revyn to move. His entire focus stayed glued to the scarf in his hands.

"Sit down." She gestured toward a small red settee. Revyn dropped onto the upholstered bench without argument. She could see clearly now that it wasn't a trick of the light. His hands were definitely shaking, and it only grew worse the longer he stared at his scarf.

Taking the blue knit accessory into her own hands, she stared at the slash carefully. If the fabric had been woven, that would have been one thing. But since her parents had been sending her away from their company to do quiet activities since she was four years old, she happened to know how to knit very well.

She glanced at him once more before she began unraveling just a bit of the slashed fabric to make the mending easier. "Your arms are very long."

Revyn jolted backward as he stared at her. "My…" He looked down at each of his arms before turning back to her. "What?"

Holding a piece of yarn in place, she reached back and opened a drawer in the table behind her. Her embroidery needles were a bit too small to be ideal for this task, but they would still work. She grabbed one and shut the drawer. "Most people have an arm span as long as they are tall. But your arms are much *longer* than you are tall. It's not unheard of. It's just a little unusual."

Instead of cocking his head, or narrowing an eye, or showing any of the signs of the confusion she expected to see, he just gulped. He stared at her for an extra long moment, and then looked away a little too casually. "You cannot possibly know how long my arms are compared to my height just by looking at me."

She shrugged and finished prepping the cut pieces of yarn in the scarf. "Most people can't, but I can. My lady's maid says my ability to estimate size and shape is a gift, but I disagree. I'm almost certain it's related to why I can't—"

Her words cut off as she realized what she had almost said. Heat trickled into the tops of her ears. Her secret. She had almost given away her most heinous secret, and to a stranger no less! Biting her lip, she leaned a little closer to the scarf and started tugging at the bottom end of it. "I think my ability to inherently know the shape and size of things causes more trouble than it's worth. I often wish I was like everybody else."

Revyn didn't respond. In fact, he didn't seem to have heard much of what she had just said. His fingers stretched forward until he barely brushed them against his scarf.

She glanced up at him with a smile. "Don't worry. I happen to be very good at mending knit fabric. This scarf is so long, I'll just take a bit of yarn from the bottom and use it to repair the cut in the middle."

He didn't look hopeful as she began unraveling the yarn from the bottom. His knee started bouncing as a look of horror filled his eyes. He kept staring harder at the scarf, as if that might help to save it.

Somehow, she suppressed the smile that kept trying to sneak across her lips. Once she had enough yarn from the bottom, she snipped it with the pair of scissors she had retrieved from the table behind her. It only took a few careful turns of the needle to tie off the end as perfectly as it had been before, even though it was now two rows shorter.

She began weaving the piece of yarn in and out of the loops at the edges of the slash. Little by little, new stitches formed that looked as neat and tidy as the stitches already there.

Revyn leaned forward each time she created a new stitch. His knee bounced higher and higher, but at least his eyes had stopped growing so wide.

Still, he watched her with palpable intensity. It was as if he were waiting for her to heal the injury of a beloved sibling, not stitch up a little cut in a plain blue scarf.

Her gaze flitted to his for a brief moment before she focused on the fabric again. "This scarf must be important to you."

His hand lifted until he held a closed fist directly over his heart. "Yes, it's…" He swallowed hard when words failed him. The fist over his heart tightened. "I need it."

Nodding, she continued her work, this time, being even more careful and attentive than before.

A subtle change came over him once she reached the halfway point. Before, nearly every muscle in his body had been rigid and shaky. But now that the scarf looked more and more like it did earlier, wonder filled his eyes.

He stared as intently as ever at the scarf, but every so often, his gaze would drift to her fingers. Awe lit his features as he watched her work, as if she performed magic.

The moment she finished and tied off the loose end, his hand came forward and brushed over the area she had repaired. He touched it with the reverence one might reserve for a newborn infant. His jaw dropped slightly as he tested the stretch in the repaired spot and found it identical to the rest of the scarf.

She had never met anyone so fascinated by such a simple repair. As someone who was usually ignored, she couldn't help basking in his awe just a little. Having someone see her, appreciate her, it felt better than opening presents, better than eating the most glorious food. For a moment, she even dared admit to herself that it felt better than any day she had ever spent in her parents' house.

His fingers fully gripped the scarf now. He tested its strength and softness. He touched it like it was the first time he had ever seen a scarf in his life. "This is…" His head shook while his jaw continued to move, as if he couldn't find the words. Letting out an amazed sigh, he shook his head again. "I can repair some things— weapons, dishes, chains—but I confess, I know nothing of fabrics. I did not think something like this was possible."

From across the room, a metal serving bowl clattered to the ground, breaking their quiet moment. They both turned to see Fritz with potatoes at his feet and bits of food at the bottom of his pant legs. He started shaking a finger at a servant, except the servant stood more than a table length away from him. Even though a serving bowl of potatoes had clearly been dropped at his feet, there was no way the servant could have anything to do with it. But apparently, that didn't stop Fritz from blaming.

Clara sighed and tucked a bit of her dark brown hair behind one ear. "Just ignore Fritz. He's always been treated as less than his older brother, which was sad when he was young. He didn't have to turn out awful because of it, though. He had good friends and an uncle who loved him more than his parents ever did. But something changed in Fritz a few years ago. Now, he seems intent on becoming the worst person alive just to prove he can."

Revyn said nothing when she finished speaking. Considering how intensely he stared at his scarf, he might not have noticed she was speaking at all. When he finally did respond, he kept his gaze on the blue fabric. "I must repay you for this. I know rules are different here, but this is too great a gift. I must."

He nodded to himself and finally looked at her. He didn't hold her gaze for long. Soon, he glanced down and around at her clothes and hair and even her hands. After a moment, his head cocked to the side. "What happened to that box you were holding earlier? Weren't you holding something when—"

His words stopped short when he glanced up at her face.

Tears already stung at her eyes, but she could feel more coming too fast to stop. Hoping to distract him, she gestured across the room toward the pile of broken porcelain.

"At least I was able to repair one of the items Fritz destroyed tonight." She sniffed as she stared at the broken gift she had spent months preparing. "The cup and saucer I painted are, sadly, beyond repair now."

As she finished speaking, the tears she had tried to hold back rebelled against her. A few drops slipped from her eyes and slid down her cheeks. She went to wipe them away with the back of her hand, but Revyn got there first.

Using his newly-repaired scarf, he caught the two tears just before they dropped off her chin. Her heart squeezed at what she assumed was a comforting gesture, but then she caught sight of Revyn's eyes.

They had opened so wide, his eyebrows nearly reached his hairline. Using one finger, he poked the wet spot on his scarf. "I have never seen anyone cry before. I thought it was a myth."

"A myth?" She sniffed the rest of her tears away. "Who's never seen anyone cry before?"

He poked his scarf again, letting his finger linger on her tears. "I come from…" He didn't seem to realize he had trailed off. After another moment, he started again. "I come from a very different land."

Since he was so transfixed by her tears, she figured he wouldn't mind if she reached toward him. Her hand brushed over the light blue and brocade overcoat covering his chest. "I wondered. I have never seen a uniform like this before."

Before he could react to her touch, she tugged the scarf out of his hands and started arranging it onto his shoulders. After only a moment, she stood and took a step back with a gasp. "You *are* as tall as your arms." She raked her gaze over his body, but it didn't give any of the answers she sought. "How?"

Any other person might have brushed it off, but not her. She knew what she could see, and she knew what she felt when she placed the scarf back onto his shoulders. Her head shook as she tried to make sense of it. "You are taller than you appear."

At the sound of those words, his face turned as white as a sheet. He clamped a hand over the scarf that was now wrapped around his neck, and then he backed away into the crowd.

She wouldn't let him get away so easily, not with such a mystery to unfold. But when she started to go after him, she found he had disappeared completely.

Her fingers clenched into fists as she scanned the room. He couldn't have gotten away so fast without her seeing. She should have been able to find his head of brown hair somewhere, or glimpse his strange uniform at the very least, but there was nothing.

It was as if he had disappeared completely. Her eyes narrowed, determined to keep looking. There was something curious about this mysterious stranger. Something much bigger than she had originally realized. And no matter how difficult it might be, she was determined to find out what.

4

Clara meandered every corner and nook of the party but failed to find Revyn the whole rest of the night. As the string quartet's music grew lazier, the raucous laughter grew louder, and the platters of food emptied, she kept hoping for a tiny glimpse of him.

A few different times, she was certain she had found him, but when she turned that way, she'd be faced with nothing. Her heart sank a little more each time it happened. With each hour she failed to find him, a little part of her remembered it was also one hour closer to the wedding that would effectively end her life.

Even opening presents hadn't cheered her like it usually did. Her parents had spent quite a bit more on her than usual that year, probably since—with her wedding the next day—they knew the neighbors would expect it.

She'd received opulent gowns, strands of diamonds and pearls, even a tea set that had been painted by the finest artist in town. Fritz and his parents also gave her gifts far more wonderful than she expected. A fine trunk made by an expert craftsman stood out as the most expensive one.

Yet none of it changed the personality of the young man she was doomed to marry. Fritz's only good qualities were ambition and cleverness, but he so often paired those with jealousy, selfishness, and greed that nothing good was left.

At the end of the evening, she tucked herself into a ball on the plush chair closest to the fire. Luckily, she nodded off and didn't have to wait while all the guests departed.

When her eyes finally fluttered open again, the guests that were staying for the night were already tucked into their rooms, and all the other guests had left.

The dark room was a shadow of what it had been earlier. All the food and platters had been cleared off the tables, leaving them lifeless and empty. The large Christmas tree stood tall, but without the lit candles, it appeared more ominous than magnificent. Even the fire next to Clara's chair had died down to mere embers.

She stretched and smoothed a few wrinkles from her pink silk gown, then trailed across the creaking wooden floorboards to see if the servants had accidently left any food out.

Only one table still held food, but it was nothing more substantial than a few snacks. Clara stood in front of the nut table, pulling a nutcracker close to her as she picked out a hazelnut with her other hand. But as she lifted the nutcracker, something behind it caught the moonlight.

Her hand trembled as she pulled the stark white object closer to her. Angling her body to allow more moonlight to spill over it, she let out a gasp.

She held in her hands the cup and saucer she had spent months painting. The purple flowers and painted gold trim looked exactly as she remembered them. Even more remarkable, they were no longer broken. The damage Fritz had done when he threw them to the ground couldn't be seen at all.

Pulling the cup closer to her face, she squinted while trying to look for a crack. Perhaps someone had glued the pieces together. Her mind immediately went to Revyn. He had said he needed to repay her for her help with the scarf. He had even mentioned he could repair dishes. But this? This was miraculous. No matter how she squinted or angled it to catch more light, she couldn't find any evidence of the pieces breaking at all.

Somehow, her nutcracker man had repaired the cup and saucer to their former pristine condition.

She wanted to cry. She wanted to shout for joy. With all the sleeping people in the house, she decided she'd just have to keep the overwhelming gratitude inside her heart where it wouldn't disturb sleeping guests. So, she simply left the cup and saucer outside Heidi's door.

It would have been better to leave them wrapped and with a tag, but even like this, surely, Heidi would guess who they came from.

After Clara set the cup and saucer outside her maid's bedroom door, she slowed her footsteps to admire the wintery world outside the large window before her.

The moon shone bright in the sky, but it would be covered by clouds soon because it had started to snow. Big fluffy snowflakes drifted down from the sky, layering over the icy, crusty snow that now covered the ground. The guests who had already traveled home would be grateful they wouldn't have to ride a carriage in such weather the next morning.

A chill slithered down Clara's spine as she examined the landscape. Something about the trees near her house looked…different. That chill in her spine multiplied when she noticed movement, not among the branches or leaves of the tree, but on the trunk.

For such an old and large tree, the trunk shouldn't have been moving at all.

Just as she gulped, she noticed the same strange movement coming from the tree next to it. Her mind screamed at her to get away from the window, to rush into her room and hide under the covers. But she couldn't listen to her mind when her feet were frozen to the floor. Fear edged into her bones like ice, freezing away the last bit of warmth she'd gotten from falling asleep by the fire.

Her thoughts turned to the other strange occurrence of that evening. How had Revyn disappeared for the rest of the night? Perhaps he had something to do with this strange movement in the trees.

Before she could consider that further, three other tree trunks began squirming and writhing. Her hand flew to her open mouth when she spied a distinct pair of eyes appear in the trunk of one of the trees. And then another pair of eyes appeared.

She realized then that the eyes weren't *in* the tree like she had originally thought. Creatures of some sort had merely disguised themselves to look like the tree trunks. But now the creatures stepped away from the trees and pulled off their disguises.

Another gasp wanted to pass through her lips, but her lungs had momentarily forgotten how to work. She couldn't gasp. She couldn't even breathe.

She'd always been good at judging heights and sizes and distances, but for the first time, she questioned that ability. Because this…this couldn't be possible.

Huge creatures moved away from the trees, each one at least nine feet tall. Their thick legs looked like architectural columns, unlike any human legs she had ever seen. And maybe it was just the moonlight, but they definitely appeared to have greenish skin. In fact, maybe it wasn't just green*ish*. Maybe it was actually green.

The creatures each held an axe, which they swung so forcefully, they probably could have chopped down a hundred-year-old tree in only three swings. When they opened their mouths, their teeth looked like rocks. And now that she looked closer… did they have grass and moss for hair?

Trolls. If she had to give the creatures a name, it would be trolls. Heidi once had a book that talked of mystical creatures like dryads, mermaids, fae, and trolls. Of all the descriptions Clara could remember, these matched the book trolls nearly perfectly.

Goose bumps ran across her skin. Her shoulders shuddered as she attempted a step backward. She managed a tiny step, despite her fear, but then the largest troll, one with granite-like skin, opened its mouth and roared.

Her feet froze again as the creature jammed one of its huge fists into a large rose bush. When its fist reemerged, it clasped a man inside it.

Clara sucked in a sharp inhale at the sight. Not just any man. Revyn. The troll had Revyn. His blue scarf waved behind him as he kicked against the troll's belly.

Revyn managed to free himself from the creature's grasp, but now all five of the trolls swung their axes toward him. He ran toward the trees. When his scarf unwrapped from around his neck, he didn't even turn. He just snatched the scarf from the air with one hand— without looking—and kept on running.

But then one of the trolls stuck out an enormous leg, which tripped Revyn. The young man would have fallen flat on his face, except another troll plucked him from the air between its enormous, rock-like finger and thumb.

They were going to hurt him. Both of Clara's hands clapped against her cheeks as she realized, no, they weren't just going to hurt him. They were going to *kill* him.

Her heart seized inside her chest. They couldn't. He had repaired the cup and saucer Fritz had so spitefully destroyed. Revyn had cracked hazelnuts for her and wiped away her tears.

The urge to ignore all semblance of logic and go outside to help him burned strong in her chest. But then another thought came that twisted at her insides.

Trolls didn't exist. No one could repair porcelain without at least a tiny crack still showing, no matter how expertly it had been glued. The nutcracker man did seem magical in a way, especially when he appeared shorter than he truly was, but perhaps that was just a strange trick of the light.

Truth hit her as heavily as the weight of her impending marriage. This was a dream. It had to be. Nothing else could explain the sight of trolls in her yard. That meant the repaired cup and saucer weren't really repaired either. The thought sent a quake through her shoulders.

Since this was a dream, there was no point in rushing to Revyn's rescue. It wouldn't change the fact that she'd never again see him in real life.

It wouldn't change the fact that her life was about to end.

Revyn produced an axe from his pocket, which only proved again this had to be a dream. An axe that large never would have fit inside a pocket. He swung it at the nearest troll and managed to slice off a bit of the creature's grassy hair, but he failed to make contact with the troll's neck.

When the swing missed, one of the smaller trolls swiped an arm across Revyn's chest, which slammed him against the ground. Even from inside the house, Clara could see the wind had been knocked out of him.

She tried not to care. She tried to remind herself this was just a dream and that the true Revyn was probably in a cozy bed, already asleep for the night.

But then one of the trolls grabbed Revyn by the ankle and yanked. Did the troll intend to rip his leg from its socket? A blood-curdling shriek erupted from Revyn's mouth.

With a knot in her chest, Clara lifted her skirts and ran for the front door. Dream or not, it didn't matter anymore. She couldn't stand by and watch such awful things happen to the young man who had been so kind to her.

Besides, if it was a dream, she couldn't be injured anyway.

An icy blast of wind froze on her skin as she threw the front doors open. As they slammed behind her and her boots hit the crusty snow at her feet, a new realization hit her.

If this truly was a dream, she wouldn't have felt the cold. But she did feel it. Somehow, she wasn't dreaming at all. But if this was real life, that meant whatever danger she was about to face was utterly and completely…real.

5

Freezing wind wrapped around Clara tighter than a blanket. The fluffy snowflakes that had looked so beautiful while inside, now landed on her arms like icy needles. Her heavy boots crunched over the landscape. Snow managed to creep above the sturdy boots and onto her stockings, which chilled her legs even more.

Her shoulders were only barely covered by her silk dress, and with her dark brown hair up in a twist, her arms, neck, and upper chest were almost entirely exposed.

If she had any doubt before, it left her now. This wasn't a dream at all. Her teeth wouldn't have been chattering if it were.

Before she could even think of turning back, she reached the yard where Revyn and the trolls still fought against each other. Somehow, Revyn had escaped the trolls' grasps, but they must have destroyed his axe in the process. It now lay with a splintered wooden handle in two different pieces on the ground.

Staying close to the house and hidden in its shadows, Clara crept closer to the fight. Her skirts gathered even more snow than her stockings did. They were soaking wet in only a few minutes. Her mother would have died on the spot if she saw how much mud already coated the hem of Clara's dress.

Now that Clara had reached the back of the house, she stood only a dozen feet away from the fight. Even though she had already seen their height from the window, she still gasped at the sight of the trolls. They towered over everything except the very tallest trees.

Revyn looked much taller than he had while inside her home, probably six and half feet. But at nine feet, the trolls' wide bodies looked capable of crushing him without much effort.

Her fingers twitched at her sides as her heart beat wildly. What was she thinking? These trolls were enormous. Maybe she had found some sort of bravery coming out to the yard, but it was useless now. What was she supposed to do against such terrifying creatures?

Biting her bottom lip, she thought about backing away. But then she counted the trolls ahead of her.

Four.

If it weren't for the ice in her bones, she would have poked her tongue into her cheek. Hadn't there been five trolls earlier?

The exact moment that thought snuck into her mind, a grip strong enough to crack a thousand hazelnuts clamped around her waist. Soon, she was swept off her feet and high into the air where she came face to face with a troll.

It breathed heavily through its squashed nose. Green, rock-like skin stood out against the mop of moss and vines atop its head. Gray eyes blinked back at her as it examined her body.

With a grunt, the creature gestured at her and then back at Revyn. "This taste better than that."

Its voice. Her insides squirmed as if worms had taken over all her muscles. *That* was its voice? She could hear the words and understand the creature, but it didn't sound like a voice. It sounded more like gurgles and coughs and oozing puddles of mud.

Across the yard, the tallest troll let out a heavy grunt. "Drop."

Clara cringed again. The second troll's voice sounded like spits and rocks scraping over a chalkboard.

Then the tallest troll jabbed a finger as thick as a scroll toward Revyn. "Kill deserter first."

Revyn had been narrowly avoiding every swing of the trolls' axes. At the sound of the spitting, rocky words of the tallest troll, Revyn scoffed. "I only deserted because my court is being held hostage by a *troll.*"

His entire face twisted over the last word, as if it were the vilest curse known to man.

A screeching laugh that somehow sounded worse than rocks scraping over a chalkboard erupted from the tallest troll's mouth. "No, stupid fae." He touched a hand to a metal circlet balancing on his hair of seaweed and coontail. "*I* king now."

After he pointed it out, Clara took a better look at the metal circlet, which was in fact a magnificent crown. The tines looked like icicles, but they caught the light like prisms. Silver formed the metal circlet shape. Soft blue fur decorated the bottom, which would have made it comfortable to wear, except the troll's head was three times too big for it. The dazzling headpiece had clearly been made for a man closer to Revyn's size.

If the size hadn't been enough to prove this troll only pretended at being king, the snickering from the other trolls confirmed it.

Before they finished laughing, one of the trolls grabbed Revyn by the forearms. As it lifted him into the air, another troll grabbed Revyn's legs. A third troll swirled its axe in a circle and then prepared to take aim.

The nutcracker man didn't seem to have any chance of escape. Even worse, the troll who had grabbed Clara still hadn't let her go, even though the troll king had said to drop her.

Revyn struggled against the grips holding him. His body writhed as he glared at the troll king standing before him. "That crown still belongs to King Pavel. Just because you stole it doesn't mean you can claim its magic. The king has to die before anyone else can take the crown." His eyes narrowed as he bared his teeth. "And we both know you aren't powerful enough to defeat the Fairfrost king."

All five of the trolls growled at those words, which sounded even worse with the added gurgles.

The troll aiming its axe at Revyn pulled it back.

But before he could change its direction and swing the axe toward Revyn, something happened that Clara only barely had the words to explain. Something erupted from Revyn's fingertips. Something iridescent and light blue. It looked like light blue smoke filled with stars, except the stars twinkled and sparked with some sort of energy she couldn't explain.

Was it…magic? She'd already accepted the trolls existed, but this was something else entirely. Could it actually be that magic existed too? And that Revyn was not just a strange and mysterious young man, but that perhaps, he was something more?

The sparkling smoke shot from his fingertips and blasted into the troll attempting to kill him. A grunt left its mouth as the towering creature immediately fell backward to the ground with a thud. More magic shot from Revyn's fingertips, dropping another troll to unconsciousness in a matter of seconds.

The troll holding Clara dropped her unceremoniously as it rushed forward to help its fellow trolls. She had to curl her knees up to her chest to keep from hurting her ankles from the fall. Crusty snow dug into her skin and soaked her silk gown.

By the time she got to her feet, the troll king was limping and another of the trolls had been knocked unconscious.

Only the troll king and the troll that had grabbed her were left. They kept swinging their axes toward Revyn with ferocity she had never seen before. But Revyn just ducked and jumped and narrowly avoided every swing while also throwing his magic at every opportunity.

She ran closer to them, still anxious to help in some way. When a troll tried to grab her again, a blast of Revyn's magic came so close, it nearly touched her nose. With a gasp, she froze on the spot.

"You all right?" Revyn said while ducking to avoid an axe swing.

"All right?" She scoffed. Of course she was not alright. She was trying to reconcile the fact that both trolls and magic apparently existed. And now that she was closer to him, she realized Revyn had pointed ears and even more stunningly handsome features than she had noticed earlier.

"Are you?" he asked again more pointedly.

Snow completely soaked her dress and more than a little mud covered it too. Her once perfectly coiffed hair now had several strands loose that brushed her shoulders and neck. Still, she'd rather fight trolls than marry Fritz. With a shrug, she nodded. "I suppose I am all right."

"Good." Holding her gaze, Revyn threw her a sly wink. Then he jumped with both feet against a tree trunk and rolled into a flip. If he meant to impress her, he did an excellent job of it. Her eyes opened wide, and her hand touched her collarbone. Even with snow falling, a tingle of heat filled her cheeks.

He sent a blast of magic at the troll who had captured Clara earlier, knocking the creature down instantly. His gaze focused as he turned his full attention on the troll king. Both of his hands lifted while sparks seemed to ignite in the very air around them. Energy crackled at his fingertips, promising the blast about to erupt from them would be even bigger, even more powerful, than any of the previous blasts.

Just as Revyn's lips started turning upward, the sound of a snapping twig came from behind him.

Before Clara could even gasp, the troll that Revyn had just knocked to the ground, quickly sat up and grabbed him.

It had been a ruse. The troll hadn't been knocked unconscious like the others. It had only been pretending. Now it yanked Revyn back, and even worse, it pinned Revyn's arms against its body. The troll then clamped its rock-like fingers over Revyn's hands.

Terror etched across Revyn's face. Clara hoped he could still shoot magic from his fingertips while they were covered by the troll's fists, but judging by the horror in his eyes, he probably couldn't. For the first time since the fight began, Revyn looked afraid.

The troll king lumbered forward with its axe raised high. The crown on its head bounced as the creature limped. Even injured, it wouldn't take the troll long to reach Revyn.

Clara's jaw clenched tight. She had to do something. This was the whole reason she had come outside in the first place. She had to help. But how?

Her eyes scanned the area around them. Snow and ice, broken tree branches and useless rose bushes surrounded them, but nothing stood out as helpful. The fallen trolls still gripped their axes tightly, but even if the axes had been available, they wouldn't be much help to Clara. She couldn't possibly swing any weapon with enough force to damage the troll's stone-like skin.

And then she saw it. The troll king teetered each time he stepped on his injured leg. The limp provided everything she needed.

Holding a breath in her mouth, she quietly ducked and ripped off her boot. She had always been good at judging distances, at knowing exact lengths and angles, at seeing all sorts of things others couldn't see without measuring.

Unlike most people, she could measure those things in her mind, which allowed her to see the one chance she had as clear as day. If she could just tip the troll to the side ever so slightly while he teetered on its injured leg, the creature would lose its balance and fall to the ground. But it wouldn't just hit the snow.

She eyed the creature and its weapon again, double-checking the measurements in her mind.

The troll king took a breath, ready to aim its axe. Clara had no time to think, no more time to measure. With all the strength she had, she threw her shoe as hard as she could straight at the troll king's head.

Her breath froze as she watched her brown boot arch through the air.

The troll holding Revyn noticed the boot almost as soon as it left her grip. It scratched its head in confusion. Even Revyn raised an eyebrow, though not in wonder. He looked more bewildered than anything.

A part of her wondered if he thought her a silly, ignorant child to think something so small could stop a nine-foot troll.

A weakness in her knees made her wonder the same thing.

But then the troll king stepped onto its bad leg, and it started to teeter. At the perfect moment, her boot slammed into the side of its head. It let out a grunt that had a fair amount of spit in it too, but then…

The entire world moved in slow motion as she watched. Her fingers curled into fists waiting, hoping.

At an achingly slow pace, the troll king leaned to the side.

But it leaned too far, too fast. Its arms swung to catch its balance, but it was too late. Just as she predicted, the creature's axe hit the ground first. But since the troll still held the axe, the curved blade pointed up.

The troll king tried to catch itself from landing on the weapon, but soon the weight of its entire body forced it down. Right onto the axe. The blade sliced into troll, directly under its armpit. The creature let out a howl that shook the trees around them. But then the cry cut off short as dark blood spilled from the wound.

Growling, the last troll tried to throw Revyn to the ground. The distraction must have loosened the troll's grip, though, because Revyn had already wriggled free of the creature's grasp. He sent a powerful wave of magic at the troll, slamming it into the ground.

This time, the troll didn't get back up again. Somehow, miraculously, the two of them had done it. Granted, Revyn had done nearly all the work, but Clara had defeated the troll king mostly by herself. She'd take that victory and hold it tight in her heart forever, even though her life was about to end tomorrow.

Once they both had a chance to take a real breath and appreciate that they actually had defeated the trolls, Clara and Revyn looked at each other. He wore an expression that said exactly what she felt, which was that she had no idea what to say or even think about what had just happened.

Since thoughts had left her mind completely, the words in her mouth came out before she could consider how they would sound. "What *are* you?"

That made Revyn chuckle. He glanced down at himself. "I must have lost control of my glamour during the fight." Shrugging, he continued. "I am a high fae from the Court of Fairfrost. I thought I could hide from the trolls here in the mortal realm, but I guess the magic that ties soldiers to my court is stronger than I thought."

None of that made any sense at all, so Clara decided to nod thoughtfully in response. Anything she said at this point would only make her look ignorant.

Revyn stepped across the snowy ground until he found his axe. Its wooden handle had been split in two.

With a few waves of his hand—and more blue magic—his axe was suddenly repaired. He then dropped it into his pocket like it was nothing more than a coin. Perhaps that took more magic.

"I must get to the Court of Crystalfall. More trolls, or even King Pavel himself will be after me eventually. Now that I can open a door outside of Fairfrost, though, I should be able to get to Crystalfall."

His hand waved in a circle and a swirling tunnel appeared before him. The walls of the tunnel appeared to be made of the same sparkly blue smoke as his magic. Scents of peppermint and pomegranate wafted through the tunnel toward them. Energy coursed through the *door*, as he called it, filling the air with crackles.

Clara might have gasped at the sight alone, but the sight combined with the scents and other sensations caused her to freeze in place instead. All she could do was stare in awe.

But then Revyn took a step toward the door, and her senses snapped back in a flash. "Wait," she called out a little breathlessly.

When he turned to glance at her, she stood taller. It took a hard swallow before she could speak again, but when she did, she filled her words with as much feeling as possible. "Take me with you."

He raised an eyebrow at her and then glanced pointedly at her house, which stood nearby. "What about your life here? If you come to Faerie, I may never be able to bring you back."

Her conviction grew as she took a step toward him. "I have no life here."

Now his head cocked to the side with a patronizing tilt. "The land I come from is dangerous."

She shook her head, rolling her shoulders back and standing as tall as possible. "You don't understand. If I stay here, my life will end tomorrow. I'll be alive, but I'll never know happiness again. All I've ever wanted was to escape. I just never thought it might be possible."

His arms stiffened as he landed his hands on his hips. "You might *die* in Faerie."

"I don't care." She turned her gaze toward her house and immediately flinched at the sight of it. "I'd rather die there than live here. I beg of you, take me with you."

Lowering his arms to his sides, he took a step toward her. His gaze slid over her, examining every part of her body. Other men had examined and enjoyed her figure before, but Revyn didn't stare in that way at all. He seemed to be taking stock in her abilities more than anything. After staring for a particularly long moment at the arm she had used to throw her boot, he lifted his gaze to hers. "You can tell how tall things are, even without touching or measuring them?"

"Yes." Her nod was probably a little too eager, but at this point, she didn't care.

He touched a finger to his chin as he stared into the nearby trees. "Perhaps you can be of use to me." After another moment of silence, he nodded once. "I propose a bargain. I will take you to Faerie, and you can stay there as long as you like. In exchange, you will help to save a tree for some Crystalfall pixies."

Her mind immediately turned to the worst-case scenario. What if she agreed to help but ultimately failed? All she'd ever succeeded at in life was disappointing people. Everyone else her age had learned to read and write, but she still struggled with it even the day before her wedding. Her head dropped as she examined her stockinged foot that no longer had a boot. "I'll try my best."

Taking a step forward, Revyn tilted his head until he caught her gaze. "You accept?"

His stormy gray eyes stared intently, sending a whirl through her stomach that flopped it in on itself. Could he tell how desperate she was? Maybe she couldn't hide how much she doubted herself, but she'd do her best to attempt it. Donning a light smile, she nodded. "Yes."

He responded with a grin that flipped her stomach yet again. "Well then, mortal." He held one hand out to her. "Come with me to Faerie."

6

IN CLARA'S WILDEST, MOST FANCIFUL dreams, she sometimes saw a forest with pink flowers in every tree. It only took one step into Faerie to realize she hadn't been dreaming nearly big enough. Her jaw would probably stay dropped for a week straight as she tried to take in the sights.

The trees before her were indeed filled with flowers. Pink flowers, purple flowers, blue, and even orange ones grew among the leaves. But they didn't have petals like the flowers she knew. These flowers were made of tiny, sparkling gems.

Light caught the bright crystals, causing glints all over the forest before her. The strings of diamonds and pearls she had received as a Christmas present from her parents would look dull compared to these exquisite jeweled flowers.

But the flora inside the trees was only the beginning. The trees themselves had trunks of gold. At first, she assumed the wooden trunks had been painted with golden paint similar to that which she had used to trim the edges of the cup and saucer for Heidi.

But after several steps and more careful examination, she realized it wasn't paint, and it wasn't a trick of the light. These trees were actually made of pure, solid gold.

By that point, the fact that the leaves themselves were not a plant but simply opulent emeralds cut in leaf shapes was almost expected.

Only the very vaguest, furthest corner of her mind registered that they arrived in Faerie in the middle of the day, even though it had been the middle of the night when they left her house.

Revyn led her toward a path running next to a river. The liquid in the stream looked more like water than the emeralds on the trees looked like leaves. But the liquid still had a sparkling quality to it unlike anything she had ever seen before. Azure blue gems appeared to tumble inside the water as it all rushed forward. Just as she caught sight of an incredible waterfall that seemed to be filled with sapphires and aquamarine gems, Revyn turned around and shot a blast of magic from his fingertips.

Instead of blue sparkly smoke, this magic came out nearly colorless but with an iridescent sheen. The magic trailed backward until it formed a sort of wall directly over the path they had just passed.

After several more steps, he shot out another blast of magic, this one white with the slightest hint of purple. The barrier would have blocked them from going back the way they had come, not that she had any intention of doing that.

The only life she had was ahead.

Once he created three more barriers, she finally turned to him with one eyebrow cocked upward. "What are you doing? I'm not planning to go back or try to escape or anything."

His head tilted to the side as a stream of sparkling turquoise magic erupted from his fingertips. He looked at his hand and then at the barrier he had just created behind them. "Oh, that is not for you. As a soldier, magic ties me back to Fairfrost Court. If I am not careful, more trolls will come after me, or even worse, King Pavel. If the king finds me, I will have to return to Fairfrost."

Nodding slowly, she dropped her gaze to the ground beneath her feet. Rich black soil formed the path. Tiny white, pearl-like pebbles dotted the soil, adding beauty to an already elegant landscape. They continued in silence, but eventually Clara found courage to ask her next question.

"So, you really are a deserter then?" She couldn't very well judge him for it, especially since she had just abandoned her family and betrothed with absolutely no regrets. She did know that—in her world, at least—deserters usually weren't considered honorable.

He showed no signs of guilt. His chin tipped up high, and he even adopted a bit of swagger as he walked. "In the other courts, fae have freedom. In Fairfrost, we are controlled. We cannot open doors without permission. There is talk that our messages will soon be controlled, too, although I have no idea how any fae, even the king of Fairfrost, would be able to control the sprites. They have politics of their own."

She'd have to ask him what sprites were later, but at the mention of them, her gaze drifted upward to the glowing green lights above them. In the sunlight and with the magnificence of so many jewels and gold everywhere, they weren't especially noticeable. But they pulsed and twirled like living creatures.

"So, it's not enough to just escape your court. You have to hide now too, is that right?"

He let out a dark chuckle. "Just because I left my court does not mean I have escaped it." But then a smile passed over his features, and he readjusted his blue knit scarf. "I already have a way to escape. But it took a bargain with the pixies to learn how to do it, and now I must help them before I can go back home to my b—"

His words cut off short. When she glanced toward him, he swallowed hard and suddenly turned away. No matter how she tried to catch his gaze after that, he stared only at the path ahead. After several steps, he threw a hand over his shoulder and created another barrier behind them.

Her heart sank a little, although it shouldn't have. It was silly of her to care at all. "Let me guess. You are engaged, too, except you're eager to get back to your betrothed so the two of you can escape Fairfrost together."

Drawing his eyebrows close together, he stared at her. He must have forgotten he was supposed to be avoiding her gaze. "What is *engaged?*"

Now her eyebrows drew together. "Engaged. To be married. It's the person you are betrothed to. A fiancé. Someone you commit to being married to at some point in the future."

The confusion on his face grew with each of the new definitions. "I do not know of any fae who has entered into any such agreement." A light seemed to spark in his eyes. "Perhaps you mean a beloved—the person with whom you are in love. I do not have one of those, though."

She had certainly never been in love with her betrothed, Fritz, but she had to admit, beloved sounded a lot nicer than betrothed. "Who is it you are returning to then? A friend? A family member? A mother or a cousin or perhaps a niece or nephew."

His head shook with a spot of laughter in his eyes. "You mortals complicate things so much more than necessary. We only use a few words to describe relations. Father, mother, son, daughter, sister, and brother. I cannot even fathom what a cousin might be."

"A brother then." Her eyes opened wide as she pointed at him. "That has to be it. When you started that sentence before you said, 'I can go back home to my b…,' and then you stopped. It is a brother, isn't it?"

Instead of answering, the blood drained from his face. He stared at her carefully as his jaw clenched tight. After another moment, his gaze broke away, and he glanced back at the magical barriers behind them. "The enchantments are ready. We need to get off the path and start to hide."

He grabbed her hand and then immediately dropped it, almost as if it had burned him. After releasing her hand, he marched away from the path and beckoned to her. Soon, they stepped across a meadow with grass made of strands of green pearls. Clovers that looked like carved jade sprouted among the grass.

Now that they moved away from the black soil, she expected the delicate pearls and jade to break under her feet. Instead, the jewels held up surprisingly well. They didn't even gather any of the mud from her boots. At least, she had taken the time to fetch the boot she had thrown at the troll king and put it back on. If the jewels could withstand the pressure her boots, they probably would have hurt her if she walked on them with only stockinged feet.

Revyn reached for her to guide her down a little hill but pulled his hand away just before he touched her. He indicated their direction without physical contact.

Lifting her skirts made it easier to watch her feet with each step. She glanced back at the enchantments before traveling far enough down the hill that she couldn't see them anymore.

"Why are we moving so far away from those enchantments? Aren't those supposed to protect you from being found?"

He shrugged. "The first enchantment will be easy to find, no matter how carefully I create it. It will not keep me hidden, not really. And once they find the first enchantment, they will find the second, and then the third, and so on." He glanced back at her now wearing that same scoundrel-like smile that had already caused her stomach to flip a few times. "But once they start following the enchantments, they will assume I am somewhere down the path covered by the enchantments."

She glanced down at the hill they had just descended. "But you aren't on that path." Now her own lips twisted up to a smile. "Clever."

Gesturing ahead, he pointed to a thicket of trees that all had pink jeweled flowers among the emerald leaves. The golden trees even had an assortment of bushes scattering across the ground. Each bush looked heavy with mulberries, though if she had to guess, the berries were probably just crystals and not actual food.

"The pixies will reveal themselves once we reach that thicket." After another step, he whispered a single word under his breath. "Hopefully."

She had to increase her pace to keep up with him now. "What will happen to those trolls by my house?"

He shrugged. "They will wake up and return to Faerie. If they do not wake before day dawns, they will be turned to stone, but the trolls have an annoying habit of being difficult to kill. I am greatly impressed you managed to slay one of them."

He kept his gaze straight ahead, and he even attempted to say the words nonchalantly, but it didn't matter. She'd already heard more than she could believe. He was *impressed* with her. The feeling of it flowed into her heart like a calming cup of tea. Maybe she hadn't known him before that day, but gaining his approval was quickly becoming one of her favorite pastimes. Maybe if she thought hard, she could find another way to impress him.

The lightness in her step turned to stone as she suddenly faltered. She reached an arm across her stomach. "But if those trolls can open doors, too, what if…" She gulped. "What if someone found them and followed them. What if another mortal entered Faerie with them just like I did with you?"

Revyn just laughed. "Why would anyone leave their home for a more dangerous place? Do you know of any mortal who would?"

Unfortunately, she did. Fritz would leave the mortal realm just as eagerly as she did. He hated his family too. Except, he'd also be angry that she tried to leave him. Even if he had no desire for her, he'd still be livid that she chose to escape their wedding. And with their wedding in the morning, he and all his family members had spent the night at her house. The fight with the trolls wasn't quiet either. Even though it was a long shot, she knew in her heart, if anyone had any chance at all of using the trolls to get to Faerie, it was Fritz.

By the time she realized Revyn was staring at her, it was already too late to hide the fear in her face. The anxiety she felt seemed to fill the space between them until it painted his features too. He stared for an extra-long moment, but then he finally waved his hand through the air.

"The trolls will awake and leave the mortal realm before any other mortals find them. And if any mortals do find them, the trolls will kill them before making a bargain."

She tried to let those words calm her, but her insides had other ideas on the matter. It didn't help that when they stepped into the thicket of trees, absolutely nothing happened.

Revyn let out a heavy sigh and spoke under his breath. "This might be more difficult than I thought."

Truer words couldn't have been spoken. In the very next second, Clara stepped forward and her foot caught on a rope. With a whoosh, both she and Revyn were caught up in a net that now hung high above the ground.

Even worse, the rope appeared to be made of steel.

7

IN ALL HER LIFE, CLARA had never been close enough to a man to feel his breath on her cheeks. It didn't matter that she was suspended in the air by a steel net. All she could think about was how the front of Revyn's thighs nestled right behind the back of hers, almost like she was sitting on his lap while also mostly standing.

Her body twisted at the waist, although his did not. It left her shoulder pressed into the middle of his chest. When she glanced up, his mouth was mere inches away, sending heat across her cheeks every time he breathed out.

This was no time at all to be distracted by the subtle glints of blue in his stormy gray eyes. But how could she think of anything, *anything,* when so much of his body was pressed up against hers. Did he feel it too? This inexorable energy that buzzed in and around and through them?

Judging by the scowl on his face, he did not. "Blasted pixies and their blasted traps." He wrapped a fist around part of the net and shook it hard. Nothing happened.

With his nose still wrinkled, he glanced down at her.

Right then, everything changed. He could feel the energy now. She could tell. Before, frustration had been etched across his features. But as soon as he made eye contact with her, his entire body reacted. His muscles went just a little tighter and then he almost melted against her. His breath caught at the exact moment she bit her bottom lip.

And then he did something she had dreamed about but never expected to experience for herself.

He leaned in.

Her heart raced at the subtle movement. Lightning flashed through all her veins. The moment ended quickly. Revyn shook his head, probably realizing what he was about to do. He jerked his head away and gripped the net again. He yanked on it like he intended to pull it down from the tree where it hung.

Of course, his effort led to no change at all.

Clara's heart still raced, leaving her skin hot and itchy. She had always known men liked to kiss and touch and do all sorts of things to women. Ever since she got engaged to Fritz, things like that disgusted her. But now, a sort of wonder filled her at the thought.

Maybe women could like kissing too. In fact, with the right man involved, maybe women could like it just as much as men did.

The heat must have been getting to Revyn too. He shook the net harder, which continued to do absolutely nothing. It caused him to bare his teeth and hiss at the thicket of golden trees around them. "Plumia!"

He only waited a beat before shouting again. "Plumia, you better get us down from here." When his shouts were met with silence, he let out a grunt. "Blasted pixies."

Magic shot from his fingertips next. The sparkly blue smoke twisted around the top of the net where it was tied to a golden branch covered in brilliant emerald leaves. Pink diamond flowers grew in a cluster just above the spot where the net was secured. It was almost like the pretty flowers were hiding something.

Her eyes squinted, but with the barrage of magic hitting the spot repeatedly, Clara couldn't make out anything useful. Maybe her time would be better spent trying to move into a less compromising position.

Edging her body to one side, she hoped to come shoulder to shoulder with Revyn. The net resisted all her attempts. After a full minute of squirming, she had merely managed to get her entire back against Revyn's front. She could still feel his legs and chest pressed up against her.

This was not better.

Heat flushed over her neck. Revyn shot magic from his fingertips even faster and wilder.

Glints of gold started falling from the sky. At first, Clara assumed it was a residual effect from Revyn's magic, but it soon became clear this was something else entirely.

Fluffy snowflakes drifted down from the sky, landing like pillows on the black soil below. But these weren't anything like the snowflakes in the mortal realm. These snowflakes were gold.

Gold! Just like the trees.

For one glorious moment, she forgot all about the legs and chest and breath on her cheeks and became completely entranced by the golden snowflakes. Some were a brighter yellow-gold and others were a deeper almost-bronze-gold. They looked as much like snow as they did like jewelry. What would happen when they melted?

Sticking one hand out through the net, she caught a golden snowflake on the back of her hand. It chilled her skin immediately but felt more cool than frozen.

Its edges started melting as soon as it touched her. By the time she brought her hand closer to her face, only half the snowflake remained. After touching it with one finger from her other hand, it melted away completely, but it didn't leave behind plain water. She rubbed the small drop of liquid over the back of her hand, which smeared a golden sheen across her skin.

Revyn stopped throwing magic long enough to glance down at her. When he saw the golden sheen on her skin, his gaze immediately jerked toward the falling golden snow. Upon seeing them, he grunted. "Seriously, Plumia? Are you are watching us right now?"

His question received no answer. Now he stuck one fist outside of the net and shook it. "Do you think this is funny?"

When no answer came again, Clara decided to ask a question of her own. "Who's Plumia?"

"She is the sugar pixie who makes golden snowflakes." With both hands, he grabbed the net and shook it hard. "Let us out of here!"

Since he had stopped shooting magic, she was finally able to get a good look at the spot where the net was tied to the tree above. So, the pink diamond flowers *were* hiding something.

Energy crackled at the ends of Revyn's fingertips as he aimed them toward the tree branch yet again.

Before any magic blasted outward, Clara twisted her body to look him in the eye. "Maybe we need to get out of here without using magic."

He looked at her like she had turned into a troll. No, not just a troll. A troll who had grown three heads.

Using one hand to gesture upward, she explained. "The net isn't tied to the tree branch like I first thought. The ends of the net are looped around that golden rod up there. You can see that it's separate from the branch. It's held in place by those pink flowers. If we can wriggle the rod free, it should release the net and us."

He started nodding even before she finished speaking. The muscles in his body flexed as he reached upward. His fingers stretched higher and higher, but his hand remained at least a foot too far away to reach the rod. "I cannot reach it."

His voice stretched over the words as he continued to extend his arms upward.

She knew what had to come next. It was the only way, but it certainly wouldn't help with their proximity issue. Maybe he could handle being so close without a problem, but could she?

The longer he stretched, the more apparent it became that they had no other choice. Proximity or not, she'd have to do what she had to do. She sucked in a little breath and finally spoke.

"If you lift me, I could probably reach the rod and wriggle it out myself."

He didn't wait a single second before wrapping one arm around the back of her thighs. But as soon as his other hand met her stomach to help balance her, his breath hitched. For one long moment, he held completely still. His fingers twitched slightly as if trying to decide if they wanted to pull away or get even closer.

"Just a little higher, and I'll be able to reach it." Hopefully now that he was in his own trance, he wouldn't notice just how shaky her words were as she spoke.

And luckily, her words did the trick. With his arms still around her, still twitching slightly, he lifted her until she was high enough.

Raising both hands above her head, she reached for the rod holding the net in place. The golden object had a cool touch and felt as smooth as polished marble. When she started wriggling the rod out, she realized this gold was just as soft as the gold in the mortal realm.

Small gouges and scratches appeared on the rod wherever she managed to pull it free. It took longer than she expected to even get the thing moving.

To Revyn's credit, his arms didn't shake at all under her weight. If they had, she might have given up and tried to think of a different way to escape. But since he showed no signs of tiring, she kept at it.

After several hard tugs, the first few loops of the net came free. Revyn had to readjust then, to keep his feet on the part of the net that hadn't been freed so that he'd be tall enough to keep holding her up. She only needed to free a few more loops and they'd tumble right out of the net. In another moment, she had it.

The rod slipped from her grasp as the freed loops of the net allowed them to drop free. Revyn held her around the waist as they fell.

It had worked.

But just before they touched the black soil, their bodies stopped. They hung suspended once again, but no net had captured them. This time, magic shimmered around them holding them off the ground.

But whose magic? At first, she suspected Revyn, but the look on his face clearly proved that theory wrong. It didn't help that fear had crept into his eyes.

Was it the mysterious Plumia who had caught them? Or was it someone or *something* more sinister?

8

After hanging suspended in the air with shimmering magic for only a handful of seconds, Clara dropped to the ground with a plunk. Her elbow ached where it landed right on a pearlescent white pebble. At least the black soil brushed away easily when she got to her feet. Not that it helped much considering her silk gown was still wet and covered in mud after the fight with the trolls.

The golden snowflakes fell faster from the sky, landing on her bare arms and face. They left behind a shimmery golden sheen on her skin, but with so many of them falling on her now, they also left behind a substantial chill.

Revyn didn't bother brushing any of the black soil from his brocade jacket or leather boots. He just stood tall and folded both arms over his chest. "We escaped from your stupid trap, Plumia. You must show yourself now."

At first nothing happened, and Clara started to wonder if this Plumia actually did exist. But then she heard a noise like tiny twinkling wind chimes somewhere near the golden tree that still held the net.

The sound started out so soft, Clara had to strain to hear it. After only a few seconds, it grew slightly louder, and then…a small creature wearing lavender appeared from just behind the tree trunk.

Once visible, the little being slowly flew toward them. The creature looked like a person, except she was tiny. She was ten inches tall at the most. The long lavender dress she wore sparkled like it had been formed from tiny amethysts. Her curled blonde hair flowed beautifully behind her. She wore a small crown of purple flowers that were probably more jewel than plant. Most miraculous of all, she had four golden wings growing from her back.

As she flew, one of her hands waved toward Clara, showering her with even more golden snowflakes than before.

Revyn rolled his eyes and sighed heavily. "You can stop that. This mortal is with me. She has agreed to help you in your plight."

At the sound of those words, the pixie stopped mid-flight and jerked her head toward Revyn. Her voice came out as sweet as a sugar plum. "She is with *you*?"

"Yes. Now leave her be. I said she agreed to help, did I not?"

Still hovering mid-air, Plumia narrowed her eyes. "And how is a simple mortal supposed to be of any help at all to us?"

Now Revyn leaned back. He lifted a corner of his mouth like he had a great secret to share.

The look did everything he intended because Plumia flew a little closer, waiting for an explanation.

By the time he finally spoke, even Clara was hanging on his words. "This mere mortal killed a troll. Not just any troll either. She killed GRokasKEn."

Judging by the gasp that erupted from the pixie, this had apparently been even more of an accomplishment than Clara had first realized.

Revyn nodded with that same arrogant smile. "We have always believed the trolls were impervious to weapons of every kind, but apparently, they have a soft spot just under their armpits. This mortal knocked GRokasKEn off his feet and then got him to land on his own axe with the axe slicing him just under the armpit."

The narrowed eyes of the pixie immediately melted away into a charming smile that she directed right at

Clara. Plumia continued to fly forward, and while she did, she stopped the falling golden snowflakes with a wave of her hand.

By the time she reached Clara, the pixie grabbed hold of her silk skirt and shook her head at it disapprovingly. "Is this the sort of fabric mortals must wear in the mortal realm? This is ghastly."

Heat climbed into Clara's cheeks as she screwed her mouth into a knot. "Well, it looked better at the beginning of the evening. Before I got into a fight with a troll."

Her finger twisted through a loose strand of dark hair that hung on her shoulder. "My hair looked better too."

"Not to worry." Plumia's face lit up with an even brighter smile. "We can fix that."

She clapped her hands and suddenly a dozen pixies appeared from behind the other tree trunks in the thicket. Some wore gowns made of jewels, some wore tunics and pants made of shimmering silky velvet. Some were male, some were female. Some had dark hair and skin, some had light hair and skin. Every color of the rainbow made up their clothing. Lavender, teal, peach, navy, magenta, and cherry. Some of them even wore colors Clara had never seen before.

As the pixies surrounded her, Revyn threw her a pointed glance. "Do not be so taken with these creatures. They are twice the size of sprites, and at least four times as mischievous. Sometimes they lead travelers to their deaths just because they think it is funny."

Plumia let out a *tsk* as she glared at Revyn. "Not just because it is funny. Their bodies fertilize the land, which brings us a more delicious harvest. And we only ever lead away the bad travelers."

Revyn shook his head and turned away. "Your definition of bad is purely subjective. Do not act as though you are bringing justice by leading people astray."

By then, Plumia had stopped listening to Revyn entirely. She pointed at three of the pixies, two females and one male, who wore marigold, rose, and garnet jeweled clothing. "Begin with the Pelo dance."

The moment she finished speaking, a song twinkled into the thicket. Clara couldn't see any instruments that created the music. None of the pixies seemed to be creating it either. The sounds simply filled the thicket, as if the air itself created it.

A sweeping melody of trumpets and flutes accompanied by strings filled the space. As it did, the three pixies flew around Clara's head. They unpinned and unbraided until her hair fell down her back. They then produced combs and some sort of oil that made her dark hair shine.

About halfway through, beautiful clacking instruments joined the trumpets with a sound that raised Clara's spirits. Soon, the pixies braided and tucked until her dark hair fell straight and glossy down to her waist. Decorative braids brought the hair away from her face in a half up, half down style she had never seen anyone in her small town wear.

The moment the pixies finished their work, Plumia clapped her hands twice and announced, "Now for the Myk'ab dance."

While the three pixies who had just done her hair joined the others, three more emerged from the crowd. A new song started too. This one had a slow, mysterious, almost haunting melody with clarinets and strings. A few tambourines joined in as the pixies worked.

The pixies produced cosmetics and immediately began applying them to Clara's face and skin. She couldn't see her face, but she did see how they smoothed the golden sheen from the snowflakes over her arms until it made her skin shine as bright as the gold and jeweled trees around her.

Once finished, Plumia clapped three times and said, "Let the Platiye dance begin."

From the music alone, Clara could already tell this dance would be her favorite. It exuded excitement and celebration. While the three new pixies worked, they also jumped and spun in the air with their wings carrying them.

The pixies started near the ground, doing some sort of magic at the hem of her skirt. Little by little, the music swelled faster and livelier, and the pixies flew higher and higher. As they worked, her stained silk dress and heavy petticoats disappeared, only to be replaced with a thick velvety fabric that felt as smooth as silk and as light as feathers.

The pink fabric had no petticoats underneath it, but it was gathered at the waist to provide for an ample skirt that flowed out all around her.

When the pixies reached her torso, the music had accelerated to a lively tempo that brought a smile to her face. Strands of white pearls formed decorative sleeves over her bare arms.

She would have given anything to admire the dress, but Plumia immediately clapped her hands four times. "Zhubao dance, make it lovely."

The music started with a bouncing tempo that was joined by a happy run done by some flutes. Three new pixies flew forward and started bouncing up and down as they created a headpiece that draped from the center top of her head and down over her braids. Strands of silver chains and pearls twinkled in the light of the thicket as the pieces came together before lightly landing on her head.

As they worked, the flutes continued with their almost bird-like song. The chorus ended by speeding up into a deeper and faster melody until it let out a long strain.

The pixies started to fly back to the others, but before Plumia could clap her hands again, Revyn groaned. "Must you pixies always be so dramatic? Are you *done* yet?"

Clara turned to him, a little more anxious than she probably needed to be. "Are you worried about how much time this is taking?"

Revyn's entire face twisted into complete confusion. He mouthed the word *time* and looked to one side, then another, as if that might give him the answer. But the longer he stood there, the deeper his confusion grew.

Plumia flew closer. "There is no time in Faerie, my dear." Now she gave a little wink. "Just one dance more. The Calceus dance."

A dancing melody featuring wooden flutes soon filled the thicket. Strings joined in the background, providing soft accompaniment.

This time, Plumia joined two other pixies as they flew toward Clara. The three of them got to work on Clara's shoes. Just like her dress had transformed, the pixies changed her plain brown boots to exquisite golden slippers with pink jeweled flowers on the top. The fabric of the shoes felt fluid and smooth, but somehow, also sturdy and strong.

She'd never know how, but if she walked into a pile of snow, she knew those slippers would stay dry.

When the last dance finished, Clara couldn't help dancing herself. She spun in a circle, watching the folds of her velvety pink dress billow out around her. The strands of pearls forming her sleeves bounced against her skin with a pleasant tinkling sound. Her luxurious hair fluttered and looked glossier than she had ever seen it in her life. Though she still couldn't see her face or the cosmetics applied there, she knew in her gut that she had never looked more beautiful.

After a few spins, she twisted herself back and caught Revyn's eye. "How do I look?" she asked as she batted her eyelashes.

To her pure delight, he blinked back at her, completely speechless. The look in his eye revealed that he liked what he saw. His jaw even dropped a little.

She couldn't help chuckling in response. Now she slid her hands over her skirt, as if smoothing wrinkles, but a magical fabric like that probably never produced any sort of wrinkles. After twirling around a few more times, she turned to Plumia.

Clara's cheeks strained from how wide she smiled. "This is incredible. I've never been treated so well in all my life. Than—"

"No!" Revyn jumped forward, suddenly grabbing Clara's wrist and pulling her closer to himself. "Do not say that."

She glanced up at his face, which had contorted into an expression of anger or possibly even fear. Clearly, he didn't understand her intention. Trying to shake herself out of his grip, she clarified. "I just wanted to tell them tha—"

"Do *not* say it." He cut her off even faster this time and then swallowed hard. "If you say those words, you will be indebted to them. Do not apologize either. *Never* apologize in Faerie."

Her eyes narrowed as she stared at his hardened glare. She realized now that he did seem to understand what she was trying to say. Her mind turned back to the party where they had first met. He cracked a few macadamias for her, and she had said *thank you*. He immediately replied with a sentence that hadn't made sense then. *You should not say those words to me.*

It had seemed strange then, but this was now the third time he had reprimanded her for offering thanks. At least this time, he had explained. If she did give thanks, that would make her indebted to the pixies. It didn't make any sense, but Revyn had been adamant that Faerie was dangerous. Maybe it was better to trust him than to take a chance.

He must have seen the moment his words sank in. His shoulders relaxed, and he let out a slow breath. These magical, beautiful pixies seemed glorious, but perhaps they were not as innocent as they acted.

After another long breath, Revyn released her wrist. "Trust me. You want to hear why they need your help before you become indebted to them in any way."

The words landed like a weight on her chest, making even the golden sheen on her arms a little less shimmery.

He turned now to Plumia. When he spoke, his words were gruff. "You need to tell her the truth."

Plumia pouted and glanced away.

Revyn just took a step closer, his face even darker than before. "All of it."

9

Jingling bells sounded as Clara started walking down a new path. Plumia flew ahead of them with her golden wings flapping as she led the way. Revyn walked beside Clara, his face dropping to a deeper scowl with each step. Each time Plumia slowed or changed directions, the quiet sound of bells changed slightly too.

After they moved away from the thicket and the other pixies, Plumia finally glanced back at them. "Everything started because Crystalfall has no leader."

When Plumia faced forward again and kept flying, Clara turned to Revyn.

He continued the story right away. "High Queen Winola, the high queen of Faerie, has chosen a king or queen for each of the other courts in Faerie but not one for Crystalfall."

Clara's golden slippers landed lightly against the soil as she nodded. "How many courts are there?"

"Seven," Plumia said over her shoulder. "Seven, including the high court. Faerie itself chose her to be high queen and then she chose leaders for all the other courts."

Clara's eyebrows rose. She wasn't sure what to make of the term Faerie *itself*, but she could worry about that later. Now her finger tapped on her chin. "That is strange, then, that she has not chosen a leader for Crystalfall."

Plumia scoffed, which ruffled her wings and tangled the sound of bells. "It is not just strange, it is dangerous."

Revyn nodded. "Since Crystalfall has no leader, King Pavel of Fairfrost thought he could take over the court and rule it himself. He took soldiers and trolls and invaded Crystalfall."

Clara's hand flew to her open mouth. "How long ago did that happen?"

Revyn's eyes narrowed. "It happened already."

"Yes, but…" Clara shook her head. "How long ago? Was it yesterday? Was it months ago? Years ago?"

He stared at her with those same narrowed eyes before turning toward the pixie. "How did you explain it earlier, Plumia? There is no time in Faerie. It just happened already. Anyway, the trolls and the soldiers, including me, attacked this court. We destroyed parts of the landscape and injured many fae creatures."

Plumia stopped flying long enough to turn around. "While he was here, King Pavel tried to create a crown with pieces of Crystalfall's landscape, so that he could become king of Crystalfall."

As Plumia turned around and began flying again, Clara laughed. "He thought if he just made his own crown, he could somehow become king?"

Both Revyn and Plumia turned to give her the exact same sidelong glance.

After she said nothing, Revyn just shrugged. "That is how things work in Faerie, except usually Faerie itself makes the crowns. No one else is allowed or able to do it, since true crowns carry enormous power. But since no one has claimed Crystalfall yet, King Pavel thought he could make the crown himself."

Clara's eyes opened wide. "So, what happened to him? Did Faerie *itself* attack him?" She wasn't sure if she used that strange term correctly, but the others didn't give any indication that it was wrong.

"Sort of," Revyn replied in answer to her question. He then glanced toward the pixie.

Plumia kept flying forward until she reached a tall tree at the top of a dip in the landscape. Once she reached the tree, she flew herself around to face the others. A hard and serious look hung in her eyes. "*We* attacked him. All the pixies did. We do not want someone from Fairfrost to rule us. Once the fight against him began, the trolls turned against him too. The trolls stole his crown and tried to kill him so they could take the crown's power. But King Pavel escaped back to Fairfrost and ordered his soldiers to return to Fairfrost too."

Revyn rubbed a hand across the back of his neck. "I *did* return as I was ordered." He raised one eyebrow. "But I made a bargain with the pixies before I left."

Clara nodded. He had already mentioned this deal before. "I remember. You learned a way to escape your court, though you haven't done it yet."

His fingers went straight to the blue knit scarf around his neck, which he glanced at twice before speaking again. "Yes, I learned how, except now I have to fulfill my part of the bargain before I can do anything else. I have to save Lifespark Tree for the Crystalfall pixies."

He stepped forward and gestured toward the dip in the land where Plumia still hovered. Following where he pointed, Clara found a small valley with a large tree growing in the very middle of it. Well, it was sort of a tree. That description didn't really fit, not in its current state.

When Revyn started climbing down the hill to the valley with the broken tree, she followed. Just like all the other trees in Faerie, this had a trunk made of solid gold. The problem was with the branches. Only a few branches were still attached to the trunk, and those all stuck out at strange, unnatural angles.

Broken golden branches with cracked and shattered emerald leaves scattered throughout the rest of the valley. Even though the trunk was gold, it looked duller than all the other trees. Every few seconds, it would pulse with a brown hue until it almost looked like a regular wooden tree trunk.

Plumia flew straight toward the tree and placed a hand on it. The moment she touched it, the tree trunk glowed with an even brighter golden glow than the other Crystalfall trees. At the same time, her golden wings gave off the same sort of glow along with the sound of jingling bells.

But the moment didn't last long. Soon, both the tree trunk and Plumia's wings dulled until they looked a sickly brown.

Plumia even lowered a little, as if her wings couldn't lift her as high as they had earlier. "This tree is the source of life for all pixies. If it stays like this, all of us will die."

Curling her hand into a fist, Clara placed it over her heart. "How are we supposed to save a tree made of gold? I assume you can't graft it like you would a regular tree."

In answer to her question, Revyn lifted one of the broken tree branches from the ground and held one end of it against the tree trunk. It didn't pass her notice that lifting such a large branch, even one made of solid gold, didn't seem to tax him in the slightest. Once he had the branch in place, he lifted his other hand and placed it flat against the tree trunk. He then whispered words she couldn't hear.

In a glow of magic, the tree branch immediately melted and stuck fast to the tree, as if it had been there all along.

Her eyes lit up at the sight. This would be easier than she thought. Her gaze scanned the valley filled with very large—and very heavy—golden branches. Then again, she likely wouldn't be much help at all. She didn't have magic to meld the branches to the tree, and she didn't have the necessary strength to lift any of them, except perhaps the very smallest ones.

Still, she chose to try her best at least. She had promised to help, after all. "Let's get to it then."

Stepping forward, she lifted a branch that was no bigger than her forearm. "Where should we put this one?" She pointed to a spot on the tree trunk. "How about there?"

With a heavy sigh, Plumia flew over to a small rock and plopped herself on top of it.

Revyn shook his head. "It is more complicated than that. We cannot put the branches wherever we want."

His fingers trailed up the tree trunk until they found the spot where he had just attached the branch to the trunk. At the spot where they merged, a line of brown sat. The brown striation worked all the way through the connection, and even though it looked a little strange, Clara realized it was probably worse than that.

Revyn continued. "We have to put the branches back in exactly the same places they were before the tree was torn apart." He sighed as he gazed over the valley filled with broken branches. "Everything has been so damaged, it is nearly impossible to tell where everything is supposed to go."

Clara realized now why Revyn was so interested in her ability to judge sizes, shapes, and lengths. This tree wasn't a new creation, it was a puzzle. All the pieces had to be restored to exactly the right place.

Luckily for her, Revyn, and the pixies, she happened to be very good at puzzles.

Her lips tipped upward in a grin. "Do we have a painting or any sort of record of what the tree looked like before it was destroyed?"

With a scoff, Revyn used magic to break off the tree branch he had just added to the tree. "I wish we did, but no."

Using one finger to draw in the black soil, Clara shrugged. "No matter." When a puzzle seemed too easy, she liked to hide the picture of how it was supposed to look and complete the puzzle without it.

Of course, *this* was not an easy puzzle at all. But difficult didn't mean impossible.

Maybe she'd just draw her own picture in the soil of how the branches should be attached. Once she got a good look at them, she could probably figure it out.

She walked around the entire valley three times, examining each tree branch. Then she circled the tree trunk five times. While she worked, Revyn grabbed tree branches at random and tried sticking them to the tree. Each time, they had the same strange brown line, indicating they were not meant to go in those positions.

So far, the tree only had two attached branches that didn't have that strange brown line, and those had probably never been ripped off in the first place.

After all her walking and examining, Clara was finally ready to try her luck at saving the tree. She pointed out a tree branch for Revyn, which he immediately lifted and brought to the tree. He held it against the trunk, but she directed him to bring it lower and over to the left. And then she told him to bring it left just a little more.

Once he finally situated it in the exact spot she imagined, she nodded. He used his free hand to release magic into the tree, which melded the two pieces of gold together.

Holding her breath, she leaned forward to check for the strange brown line. Revyn leaned forward too.

Her heart skittered as she searched, and then its pulse jumped as she realized it had worked. The branch connected to the tree without the line of brown. She had already started to save this tree, and she did it on her first try too.

Plumia clapped her hands together in delight. Revyn grinned.

They both watched eagerly as Clara picked out the next branch. When she told Revyn where to place it against the tree, he didn't complain at all as she directed him to bring it higher and to the left, then down a little and to the left a little more, and then—no, a little higher again.

When she was finally satisfied, his magic once again melted the branch to the tree. But this time it didn't work.

Her heart dropped at the sight. Revyn's shoulders sagged. Trying to stay positive, she told him to take it off. She'd seen another branch she had also thought might go in that spot.

But that one didn't work either. It soon became abundantly clear that this task would not be as easy as she had hoped.

Still, they continued to work. What else could they do?

Plumia groaned and buried her head in her hands, sitting again atop a small rock. "If only we had a leader for our court. If we had a king or a queen, the power from their crown would surely be able to fix our tree."

As she spoke, the tree pulsed and turned a little browner. Her head buried deeper in her hands.

Clara glanced at the pixie while pointing out the next tree branch to try. As Revyn lifted it and brought it near the tree, Clara whispered to him. "I do not understand why you worried so much about me being indebted to the pixies."

He kept his voice low while answering. "In Faerie, once a bargain is made, it cannot be undone. Faerie itself will compel you to finish what you have promised, no matter what. If you were indebted to the pixies, they would make you promise to save this tree. And if you made such a promise, you would die before you broke that promise. For the whole rest of your life, you would be able to do nothing else except attempt to save the tree."

A weight pressed down on her shoulders as his words sank in. She swallowed hard. "But I did promise. I made a bargain with you." If she had known that while in the mortal realm, would she have agreed to the bargain still?

In truth, she would have, and she knew it. Anything would be better than another day in the mortal realm.

After that thought eased some of the weight off her chest, she caught a glimpse of Revyn's face. Somehow, his expression eased even more of the weight off.

He spoke while attaching the branch to the tree trunk. "Our bargain was different from the promise the pixies would have required of you. Our bargain states that you will *help* to save the tree. If you attempt to save it and fail, you still helped and thus have fulfilled your duty. You will be free once you try to save it. You may even be free now since you already helped get one tree branch correctly attached."

The weight on her chest drifted away completely, leaving her feet as light as feathers. But then an entirely new weight tangled in her gut. Her gaze found his stormy gray eyes. "What about you? Will you be free if you help but ultimately fail?"

His answer was simple but heavier than the entire golden tree before them. "No."

It was clear then. He had a way to escape Fairfrost, so he and his brother could be free of the control they experienced there. But he couldn't do it until this tree was saved. Entirely saved.

Maybe her bargain with him didn't require it, but she was determined to work until then anyway. He had rescued her from her dismal life in the mortal realm. Bargain or no bargain, honor required she stay by his side until he was free as well.

Just like he had to repay her for repairing his scarf, she now had to repay him for taking her away from the mortal realm.

But sometimes, determination wasn't enough to accomplish a task. She knew as much from all her years of trying to learn how to read and write. The thought seemed darker now that the sky had darkened too. The sun had just dipped below the horizon, leaving behind a dusky gray night. And now, it seemed things were about to get a lot more complicated.

With a loud *thunk*, an axe landed in the center of the tree trunk. A moment later, three trolls appeared at the top of the hill.

Clara's heart pounded. How could they save the tree when they'd have to fight again just to stay alive?

10

Even though Clara had only seen them for the first time the night before, the sight of trolls still filled her with despair. She jumped behind the golden tree trunk, knowing it would do nothing since the trolls had probably seen her already.

They let out gurgling shouts that rippled through the air. When they charged down the hill, each of them wielded an axe. The axes looked even bigger than the ones they'd had in the mortal realm. These new ones appeared to be as heavy as the golden branches littering the ground.

When they had traveled halfway down the hill, Plumia flew off her small rock and whistled. The sound of that whistle pulsed in the air, completely drowning out the trolls' shouts. A split second later, dozens of pixies in glittering clothes flew toward the lumbering creatures.

The pixies shot magic and jewels at the trolls. The nine-foot-tall green creatures were completely unaffected as they kept charging down the hill. After their first attempt failed, the pixies threw jewels straight into the trolls' eyes. They also used their wings to fly in circles around the trolls' heads. Each of the flying creatures also shouted and screamed.

The trolls didn't seem bothered by the screaming, but the jewels thrown into their eyes and the zooming pixies flying in circles around their heads did aggravate them. The trolls started swatting at the creatures.

When one of the trolls caught a pixie in its fist, it immediately squeezed its fist tight. When it opened its fist again, the pixie fell to ground, broken and covered in dust from the crushed gems that once formed his clothing.

Clara gasped at the sight of the dead pixie. None of the other pixies stopped though. They flew in circles around the trolls' heads even faster than before. Their screaming grew more incessant. They threw gems at the trolls' eyes with more vigor.

It slowed the trolls down, but it didn't stop them. Worse, the trolls managed to kill several more pixies before they reached the valley.

By the time they arrived at the bottom of the hill, Clara had emerged from her hiding spot behind the tree. She didn't have much of a plan. To be honest, she didn't have any plan at all. But if those pixies could be brave and sacrifice so much to try and stop the trolls, then Clara would do her best too.

Revyn stood on the other side of the tree from her. Once the trolls drew near them, he shot a blast of magic from his fingertips. The smoky, sparkling magic hit the troll on the soft skin just under its armpit.

That was supposed to be the troll's weak spot, but this troll merely flinched at the contact.

Even as the troll lumbered toward her, Clara examined the creature's soft spot. It certainly did look less rock-like in that spot compared to everywhere else on its body. From what she could see, it made sense it was a weak point.

But when Revyn shot another wave of magic at the spot, the troll only flinched at it, just like before. Maybe trolls couldn't be killed with magic then. Just like magic couldn't free Clara and Revyn from that net, maybe they needed something solid. Maybe they needed a weapon.

Just as she came to that realization, another one donned just as quickly.

She didn't have a weapon.

She had a fantastic dress, beautiful shoes, and gorgeous, glossy hair, but she had nothing that could come close to piercing a troll's skin.

At this point, her only idea was to trick the creature.

The nearest troll charged Revyn, but the second nearest one charged her. She carefully edged herself to the side until she stood directly in front of the tree. Then she raised both hands and shook them the way children did while taunting each other. "Try and get me if you can. You'll never catch me. That's my plan."

As she hoped, the troll let out an incensed roar and charged even faster toward her.

Revyn had made contact with the first troll, already fighting it, but he still opened his eyes wide at her words. Then he shook his head as if she had just spoken her last words and there was nothing he could do to save her.

Maybe she *had* just spoken her last words. Taunting a nine-foot-tall troll didn't exactly top the list of ways to stay alive. But with such a large creature running so fast now, it would be nearly impossible for it to slow that momentum to a stop.

She dug her golden slippers into the black soil beneath her feet, still wiggling her fingers in that taunting shake.

The troll was five feet away from her. Four feet. Three. It reached out, nearly plucking her off the ground.

That was the moment. Holding her breath, she ducked and rolled to the side.

Before the creature could stop, it rammed its head directly against the tree trunk that had been standing right behind her.

A loud sound rang out as the stone-like troll head rammed against the golden tree. The creature left a deep dent in the trunk as it slumped to the ground.

As a highly malleable metal, gold could be shaped and scratched easily. But it was also heavy. A rock could easily dent gold, but if the rock hit hard enough, the gold could crack it.

The huge troll rolled onto the ground, letting out spits and hacks that were obnoxious and repugnant at the same time. It hadn't been nearly as injured as Clara had hoped, but it had done some good at least. When the troll got to its feet, it tumbled and tipped on every step. She had only succeeded at making the creature dizzy, but that was still a victory. Without a weapon, it was the best she could do.

While the troll stumbled and tried to catch its balance, Revyn came rushing toward it with an axe in his hand. His gaze was so focused on the soft spot under the troll's arm that he didn't even notice when a third troll struck a leg out to trip him.

The two uninjured trolls closed in around him while the dizzy troll grabbed onto the golden tree for balance. The pixies continued to scream and fly around to distract the trolls, but it didn't help much.

Revyn held his axe high, but he had little hope against two trolls at once. Sure enough, only a moment later, one of the trolls grabbed his axe and threw it to the ground.

Clara scanned the landscape for something, anything, that might help. She caught sight of a small golden tree branch with a nice point on one end. Snatching it off the ground, she shouted Revyn's name and tossed it to him.

With the pointed tree branch in one hand, he immediately slammed it into the soft skin under the nearest troll's arm. The troll used its other arm to slam Revyn to the ground while also letting out hair-raising shriek.

Apparently, the trolls really did have a weak spot just under their armpits. It hadn't been unique to the troll king. But though the troll was injured, this injury hadn't been large enough to kill it.

A small trickle of blood dripped from the wound, but it still seemed as capable as ever at fighting. With Revyn on the ground, the troll shoved a foot onto his chest. Then the troll pressed down.

Revyn's face immediately turned bright red. He gasped for air.

Clara tried to stand and run toward him, but another troll grabbed her by the waist and lifted her off the ground. "Revyn!"

She shouted his name, but he made no indication that he had heard. He just sputtered and coughed, still desperate to get some air.

The troll probably would have killed him except a voice sounded from the top of the hill. "Forget them. Get the branches. Don't you remember our plan?"

It was worrisome to hear the trolls had someone directing them, that they had a plan. If only that were her only surprise. Sadly, it was worse than that. So much worse.

Just as the troll holding her dropped Clara to the ground, she glanced up at the top of the hill. With his golden hair atop his head, Fritz stared down at her with a wicked smile. "Yes, yes. Forget them. Just get the branches like we talked about."

The trolls stopped fighting right away and started gathering branches into their arms. The pixies screamed and started throwing their own bodies against the trolls' eyes. It didn't help. Nothing helped.

Soon the three trolls had each gathered armfuls of the branches. They ran back up to the top of the hill and disappeared through a swirling Faerie door. When they left, they took Fritz with them.

Clara wrapped her arms around her stomach and fell into a heap on the ground. Somehow, Fritz had found a way to Faerie. He had clearly made some deal or other with the trolls. And now the trolls had the branches she and Revyn needed to save the pixies' tree.

Her gut churned. They were doomed.

11

THIS WAS CLARA'S FAULT. HER chin trembled as she stared at the darkened valley, now much emptier of the tree branches that had once been scattered there. Her legs curled up against her chest as she tried to calm the heaving breaths that shook through her.

If only she'd had a weapon. If only she'd been fast enough to stab the trolls as soon as they reached the valley, instead of trying to be clever and tricking a troll to slam into a tree instead.

Her head sank beneath her arms as an even greater truth rang in her mind. If only she'd learned how to read and write. If she had, her parents would have loved her. If they'd loved her, they wouldn't have forced her into an engagement with Fritz, and then he wouldn't have been offended by her rejection of him. He wouldn't have found a way to Faerie. He wouldn't have made a plan with the trolls.

It didn't help to squeeze her legs closer to her body. It didn't help to rock herself back and forth. She had only just met Revyn and the pixies, and somehow, she had already ruined everything for them.

She always ruined everything.

Her parents liked to point that out as often as they could. Heidi usually tried to pretend they were wrong. Clara usually tried to pretend to believe her lady's maid. But deep down, she knew the truth…that she failed at everything she tried. So why even try?

"Are you crying again?" Revyn's voice came out soft, though not at all gentle. He poked her with one finger and then gawked at her once he caught sight of her face.

Using the back of her hand, she wiped away her tears. It wouldn't do much good because new tears would probably join them soon. And now she had probably ruined all the nice cosmetics the pixies had applied.

"Get up." Revyn held a hand out to her, but immediately retracted it. He clasped his hands behind his back and began pacing the valley with the broken pixie tree.

His eyes closed as he walked. "I know in which cavern those trolls live, but they will fight anyone who tries to enter. Regardless, the cavern is likely where they took the tree branches."

He continued muttering to himself as he paced, as if he had forgotten Clara even existed.

While he walked, Plumia flew toward Clara and gave a loud *tsk* at the sight of her face. The little fae creature waved a hand and shot magic toward Clara's face.

A tickling feeling broke out across Clara's skin, as if tiny bubbles popped across its surface. After a few seconds, the feeling stopped and Plumia gave a satisfied nod.

The pixie flew toward a large branch and rested on the ground next to it. "Who was that mortal boy? You acted as though you recognized him."

Just like that, the churning in Clara's belly returned. Tears pricked at her eyes, but she was determined to keep her tears back, if only so the pixies didn't have to fix her makeup again. Scowling at the ground, she answered. "He's a troublemaker. Someone who could have the entire world and still not have enough."

Plumia nodded knowingly. "He fits in well with the trolls then. I am not surprised he made an alliance with them. The mortal probably thinks he has the upper hand, but any bargain with a mortal and a fae—even a troll—will nearly always favor the fae. It takes a very clever mortal to turn things in his favor."

Two thoughts struck Clara at the exact same moment. First, she knew a little too well that Fritz had always been clever, especially when it came to deals. If any mortal could make a bargain with a fae and still come out on top, it was him. Second, she had also made a bargain with a fae, except her fae had purposefully given her an easy way out.

According to Revyn, her part of the bargain was likely already fulfilled, even though the pixies were in an even worse situation than ever.

At that moment, Revyn stopped pacing and let out a huff. "Do either of you have any ideas?"

Now sitting up, Clara pulled her knees closer to her chest and wrapped her arms around them. Her voice would make it clear just how miserable she felt, but right now, she couldn't be bothered to care. "Maybe we should just give up. Sometimes determination isn't enough to accomplish a task."

Revyn scowled at the words, but after another moment, a spark lit in his eye. He raised one eyebrow and even cocked a tiny smile. "If determination alone is not enough, it simply means you are trying to solve the wrong problem. We just have to figure out the right problem, and then we can succeed."

As he spoke, the night sky turned even darker. Stars hadn't yet appeared in the sky, but they would probably be visible soon.

Plumia flew over to them, her wings giving off the sound of ringing wind chimes as she did. "No more work tonight. When night falls, the revels begin. If Lifespark Tree is to die and our lives to end, we have every intention of making the most of our evenings."

When she flew off, following a different path than the one they had arrived on, Revyn followed her with a slight glare. "We need to sleep too. We can revel for part of the night, but we will need rest if we have any chance of saving your tree."

Clara didn't have time to wonder what a revel was. By the time the question started in her mind, they had already walked straight into one.

Twinkling lights filled the gold and emerald trees surrounding them. Unlike the flickering candles that lit her Christmas tree back home, these lights didn't seem to need any fuel to stay alight. They just glowed and winked like bright spheres of white.

Long tables lined the sides of a large open space. Each table had dozens of golden plates and goblets strewn across them, though as far as she could see, they had no food.

Fae of all shapes and sizes danced in the large open area before her. Remembering the book from Heidi that identified trolls, Clara now identified several more fae creatures. Little brownies with floppy ears and wide eyes danced. Gnomes with long beards and black, bug-like eyes sang along with the music that filled the space.

Dryads floated across the black soil with the grace of royalty. Clara also spotted nymphs, satyrs, and of course, several pixies wearing colorful jeweled clothing.

High fae danced and laughed throughout the revel too. They looked mostly human, but like Revyn, they had pointed ears, inhumanly-tall heights, and more-than-perfect facial features. She could have spent the entire night staring at them. She probably would have, except her stomach had other ideas.

Revyn and Plumia followed her until she reached the nearest table. A part of her had hoped the meal would be visible once she got there, but sadly, it was not. Taking a plate from the table, she glanced back at the others. "Is there no food?"

"What food do you want?" Plumia asked with a grin.

Clara shrugged. "Anything."

Revyn shook his head. "No, you must think of something specific."

In response, Clara said the first thing that came to her mind. "Cake." The moment the word left her lips, an exquisite piece of cake appeared on the plate in her hands. Moist chocolate cake with three layers sat before her. Pink frosting held the layers together. Two plump cherries adorned the top of the slice.

Using the fork that had also magically appeared, she dared to take a bite. As she hoped, it was her very favorite flavor of cake, Black Forest. She shoveled the chocolate, cherry, and cream dessert into her mouth, not even worrying about how her appetite might be spoiled if she consumed sweets before a meal.

While she ate, Revyn disappeared to the other side of the revel. Perhaps he wanted to find a place to sleep, since he had been so intent on resting.

She, on the other hand, had absolutely no intention of sleeping. At least not until her belly was full. Grabbing a golden goblet from the table before her, she named her favorite drink out loud. Hot cider.

In less than a second, the steaming beverage appeared in her goblet. She took a long swig and didn't even wipe away the line of foam it left behind above her lips. Now that she had finished her cake, she decided to try something a little less sugary.

She conjured roasted pork and potatoes, her stomach feeling fuller by the minute. In the mortal realm, eating so much would have made her dress tight. But the pixie-made Faerie dress must have been magic and adjusted with her. Or perhaps it was the food that was magic, helping her to feel full without actually making her so.

Plumia had disappeared by then, but Clara didn't mind. Now she wandered the edge of the party looking for the source of the music. Her parents' Christmas party had boasted a string quartet with some of the finest musicians in town, but this Faerie revel seemed to have an entire symphony. Just like when the pixies had done their dances, the music didn't have any obvious source. Instead, it seemed as if the air itself pulsed and swelled with the sweeping melodies.

Someone caught Clara's hand just then. A female fae with dark skin and silver and black eyes beckoned her toward the middle of the dance floor. At the female fae's side, a male fae with orange hair and matching freckles beckoned Clara forward too.

Her eyelids had finally started drooping, but perhaps she could manage just one dance. The male and female fae closed in on either side of her, giggling as the music played. After that first dance, Clara was ready to drop from exhaustion.

She tried to sneak away and, hopefully, find Revyn. But the male and female fae just smiled and told her to keep dancing. Her mind said to leave, yet her feet kept moving. Clara tried again to get away. She really did need some rest now.

Still, her feet skipped and hopped and twirled to the music. Her head started spinning too. A third song began, and now she wanted to cry. She couldn't stop. No matter how she tried, her feet kept moving. Her heart raced faster now. It raced so fast, she could barely catch her breath.

The male and female fae who had lured her onto the dance floor laughed. At first they had laughed like they were enjoying the music and the party. Now they laughed at Clara, at her plight.

Clara's stomach wound into tight knots. Her feet ached, probably growing blisters. A single tear slipped down to her chin, but she couldn't stop. She couldn't stop, and the fae around her just kept laughing.

If her heart had been beating just a little slower, she would have called out for help. Surely, Plumia or Revyn would have been able to get her off that dance floor.

Her stomach sickened at the thought. She realized now that Plumia had led Clara to this revel in the first place. Maybe this had been her plan all along. And hadn't Revyn abandoned her almost immediately after they arrived at the revel? Maybe he didn't care what happened to her now that her part of the bargain had been fulfilled.

Just as a second tear escaped her eye, someone grabbed the male fae with orange hair and yanked him backward.

"Release her." Revyn practically growled the words at the male fae.

The male fae just laughed and clapped his hands together. "But look at how her eyes fill with fear every time she twirls. Mortals are too much fun to play with."

But Revyn didn't accept that as an answer. He drew a sharp axe from his pocket, and in a single swipe, cut off the male fae's entire arm at the elbow. Blood poured from the wound, dropping in heavy splashes onto the black soil below.

With his hand still gripping the other fae's shoulder, Revyn leaned closer. "Release her now, or I will cut off your other arm too."

The male fae pouted. He looked more inconvenienced than horrified by his detached arm. He clicked his tongue and used his free arm to cover the wound. After another moment, Clara was free.

Her feet stopped suddenly, though her heart still raced. She had to gasp just to catch her breath. As soon as she had gulped in a few breaths of air, Revyn took her by the hand and led her away from the revel.

Aches stung her feet with each step. Her magical golden slippers had kept her feet comfortable all day and night, right until the dancing began.

Still holding Clara's hand, Revyn glanced back at her. "I forgot to mention, most fae are not kind to mortals." One of his eyes narrowed as his head tilted to the side. "Actually, most fae are not kind to anyone but especially not to mortals."

When he finally stopped, he had led them to a quiet thicket of golden trees far from the party. A makeshift bed with velvety blankets sat before her. "You can sleep here. Plumia is in the tree above. I will sleep down the path a little where I will have a better view of the road."

He waited until she climbed under the blankets, which were warmer and softer than she expected. After getting comfortable, she looked up at him through her eyelashes. "Why couldn't I stop dancing?"

After letting out a sigh, he knelt down next to her. "They enchanted you. Perhaps you need a ward to protect you from fae enchantments. Plumia can probably make you something."

Now that he was eye level, Clara found it nearly impossible to pull her gaze away from his. She might have been embarrassed by it, but he seemed to suffer from the same affliction. She swallowed hard. "I can't believe you cut off that fae's arm just to protect me."

Revyn waved it off. "The arm will grow back eventually. I probably should not have left you like that, though."

Her heart skipped at the words. Now that she sat, her feet already felt better, but that hadn't stopped her heart from racing. And twirling. Even in the dusky light, she could barely make out the glints of blue in the storm of Revyn's gray eyes.

He reached for her face, brushing his thumb across her cheek.

Her breath caught in her throat. When he opened his mouth again, she could see nothing but his lips.

"I will ask Plumia tomorrow to make you a ward."

Clara nodded because she couldn't possibly speak. But she nodded with her eyes, afraid that if she moved her head too much, Revyn might stop stroking her cheek.

He held her gaze for another moment, and then he did it again. He leaned in.

No magical symphony could have played music as brilliant as the music in her heart at that moment. Nearly all the years she should have been dreaming of young men, she'd instead been dreading a marriage that would have killed her.

Now it seemed like all the years she should have been yearning came rushing back. The force of the yearning tilted her chin up. She leaned closer. One more inch and their lips would touch.

But then Revyn dropped his hand, stood up, and took several steps back. He cleared his throat and turned away. When he did speak again, his voice came out colder than an ice storm.

"Plumia said a king or queen would have the power to save the pixie's tree. I have decided that tomorrow, we must go to High Queen Winola and beg her to choose a leader for Crystalfall immediately."

He stepped even farther away, stomping a little as he did. "We leave as soon as day dawns."

12

A RED BRACELET FILLED WITH fae magic wrapped around Clara's wrist. Plumia promised it would prevent any fae from enchanting Clara again. The pixie had also used some sort of magic on Clara's sore feet, making it easy to walk when they started out the next morning.

Those kindnesses might have felt better if Revyn had bothered to acknowledge Clara's existence. He hadn't even woken her up in the morning, instead sending the pixie to do it.

Now, Clara walked at the back of a group of sixteen fae who all headed toward the high court to make an appeal to the high queen.

A female fae with long dark hair that fell to her mid-calves opened a door for them. The swirling tunnel looked nothing like Revyn's had. This new Faerie door had swirls of orange, pink, and maroon, and it smelled of cinnamon and cardamom.

Apparently, Revyn had to avoid opening his own doors or it would be easier for the trolls or the king of Fairfrost to find them. Though with Revyn at the very front of the group, doing his best to avoid Clara, she was starting to not care so much about his well-being.

They had shared such a special moment the night before. He had even saved her from those cruel fae who made her dance without stopping. And now, he found her presence unfit for his attention. It wouldn't have hurt so much if her own parents hadn't done the same thing once they realized Clara would never learn to read.

On the other side of the door, they entered a forest similar to those in Clara's world. But even though these trees were wooden and had true leaves, the lush forest still had a magical quality unlike anything she had ever experienced. Moss covered tree trunks and rocks. A light breeze kept the air cool and comfortable. The scent of crisp rain and wild berries hung thickly in the air.

Such a beautiful landscape made it difficult for Clara to keep scowling. As their group headed toward the castle, Clara also had one thing to be grateful for. She had Plumia to talk to.

Turning to the pixie, Clara tucked a strand of dark hair behind one ear. "There are people of many different colors here in Faerie. My world has people of many different colors too, but where I live, everyone mostly has fair skin and light hair. My father and I have darker hair than almost everyone I know."

Plumia flapped her wings a little faster, which made the twinkling bell sound that accompanied them ring a little faster too. "Crystalfall is different from the other courts in Faerie. In the other courts, all the fae are the same." She gestured toward Revyn, who was barely visible at the front of the group. "In Fairfrost, the fae mostly have fair skin and light-colored eyes. In Swiftsea, they have dark skin and black hair. In the high court, as you'll soon see, the fae have light brown skin, but it has a reddish undertone." She gestured now to the female fae with long dark hair who had opened the door. "In Dustdune, the fae also have light brown skin, but theirs has an olive undertone. The other courts have their own look too. Each court is different, but the fae within each one look similar to each other."

Clara turned to the side. "So why does everyone in Crystalfall look like they've all come from different courts?"

"Because they have." Plumia shrugged. "You might say Crystalfall is a court of misfits. Fae go there because they do not fit in with their own court. My court attracts mortals, too, mostly the ones who want to escape the fae who brought them here. Every high fae in Crystalfall lived at a different court at one point in their life."

Shaking her head, Clara considered the words. "But you said you did not want King Pavel of Fairfrost to rule Crystalfall. You said you did not want anyone from Fairfrost ruling the court."

"That is true."

Now Clara looked at the pixie a little more intensely. "But if Crystalfall has no natural citizens, if every fae who lives there originally comes from a different court, then who could possibly be chosen to rule it?"

Plumia winced at the words. She had probably thought of the same questions but chose to keep them unspoken. But she couldn't avoid them now. Not with them thickening the air.

Finally, Plumia released a long-suffering sigh. "The high queen will know. She chose rulers for all the other courts. Certainly, she can choose one for Crystalfall as well."

Her words were sure, but her tone was not. Plumia must have had just as much uncertainty about this appeal as Clara did.

By the time the large castle came into view, its high towers stretching to the sky, Clara's heart only scampered and twinged. Fae soldiers with light brown skin, black hair, and suede coats and pants led their group through a maze of castle hallways until they reached the throne room.

When they entered the large room, Clara's eyes widened. The vaulted ceilings appeared to be at least four stories tall. Tapestries decorated parts of the wall, running from the very top all the way to the stone floor below. A large chandelier made of white crystal hung over the center of the room. It boasted workmanship only the finest craftsman could have claimed.

At the side of the room, a man of about twenty-six years stared at the chandelier like it was as precious as his own child. After a long look at the chandelier, he then glanced at the woman sitting upon the throne. His look changed to complete and utter awe. The man appeared to be mortal. He didn't have the stunning features or pointed ears of the fae. Apparently, that didn't stop him from admiring the high queen like she was the greatest gift any realm had ever known.

Soon, their group reached the throne, which was made entirely of tree branches and the brightest, lushest leaves Clara had ever seen.

High Queen Winola had light brown skin with a reddish undertone as Plumia had described. The high queen also had glossy black hair that fell to her waist. She wore a suede dress with red and white strings of beads decorating the bottom hem. Her crown was made of small tree branches and had a green gem at the front.

Most surprisingly of all, the high queen looked no more than a year or two older than Clara. After seeing the reverence the other fae gave when speaking of her, Clara had expected the woman to be at least forty.

Instead, she appeared to be a very young adult, just like all the fae standing in front of Clara now.

The high queen didn't bother speaking a single word. She just lifted her chin and stared down at their group. Everyone instantly knew it was time to explain.

Revyn dropped to one knee. "My queen." He cleared his throat before continuing. "Crystalfall has no leader."

A flash of emotion that looked very much like anger sparked in the high queen's eyes. Despite her youth, she looked every bit like the most important person in the room. "I am aware." Her voice dripped with a patronizing tone. "You hardly needed to come all this way just to point that out."

Revyn gulped loud enough that Clara could hear it even from the back of their group. Still, he lifted his chin. "Crystalfall is also in danger. The tree that gives life to pixies has been damaged. If it is not saved soon, the pixies will die."

The slightest twitch lifted one of the high queen's eyebrows. She leaned forward ever so slightly. "And?"

Revyn continued. "We are here to ask that you choose a leader for Crystalfall." He gestured behind him at the group of fae. "Some of the court's most prominent fae are here for you to choose from."

In a graceful, sweeping motion, the high queen stood from her throne and glided over to the fae. The colors in her eyes swirled and pulsed, as if they carried magic the rest of Faerie did not have. Her chin remained high as she looked over every fae in their small group. Some fae received a closer examination. Others were only given a small glance before she shook her head and moved on.

She spent considerable time looking at Revyn. The high queen's eyes changed from dark to light and from shiny to sparkling, all in a single moment. She continued her search, even sparing a glance at Clara.

While High Queen Winola's gaze fixed onto Clara, the high queen finally spoke again. "I have often wondered who would become leader of the elusive Court of Crystalfall."

Her gaze sharpened, and her eyes swirled with more magic than ever. But then she trailed back to her throne and sat down. With a heavy sigh, she looked at Revyn again. "I cannot do it."

Even from her position behind the others, Clara could see that Revyn was taken aback. He opened and closed his mouth a few times, probably trying to figure out what he should say next. When he looked up at the high queen, she just shook her head.

"I cannot choose a leader for that court. It is not for me to decide."

One of the fae from their group stepped forward and nodded once at the high queen. "But, my queen, you chose leaders for all the other courts."

She started nodding even before the fae had finished speaking. "Yes, but Crystalfall is different. Only Faerie itself can choose leaders for it."

By now, Revyn had gotten to his feet. "Then can you save the pixie's tree? Surely, your magic as high queen has enough power for it."

"It does, but…" Her head lowered until she stared at her lap. "I cannot do that either. A way to save the tree has already been provided."

"What way?" Plumia asked. She flew closer to the throne and held her breath, waiting for the answer.

But the high queen didn't look at Plumia. Instead, High Queen Winola's gaze turned back to Clara's. "You must discover it on your own."

Breaking her gaze, the high queen waved their group off. It didn't require a single word for them to know they had been dismissed. Soldiers wearing suede immediately surrounded them and escorted them from the throne room.

Just before Clara exited the doors, she caught one last glimpse of the high queen. The woman threw a sly smile at the mortal man who had been admiring her earlier. He responded by visibly melting on the spot.

As sweet as the interaction was, it didn't change Clara, Revyn, or the pixies' plight. Without the high queen's help, they were right back where they had started.

They had a tree to save, and they no longer had the branches to do it.

13

After clara and the small group of fae left the high court and returned to Crystalfall, it didn't take long for all the other fae to go their separate ways. Still, even after only Clara, Plumia, and Revyn remained, Revyn still avoided her gaze.

He paced and kept glancing down a path of black soil and pearlescent pebbles. She had no reason to stop him from pacing. She didn't have any ideas either.

They had to get the tree branches back from the trolls. She also needed to draw a picture in the valley floor that would show which branches to put where on the tree. Even with the branches gone, she had examined them closely enough that she felt confident she could draw a decent picture. It would certainly be better than no picture like they had now.

But the picture would only help once they got the branches back. Stealing back the branches had to be their first goal. That much she knew for certain, but she knew basically nothing else. At least Revyn knew where to find the trolls. Then again, if the trolls would fight anyone who entered their cavern, they might need more help to steal the branches back.

The pixies would be willing to help, but they didn't have enough strength to do much against the trolls. And so far, the other fae Clara had met would never agree to risk their own lives unless it provided some big reward for them. But if it were that simple, the pixies probably would have gotten the help they needed already. More likely, they didn't have anything enticing enough to tempt the other fae to help them.

All at once, Revyn stopped pacing directly in front of Clara. Since they were still far from Lifespark Tree, she expected him to open a door to bring them closer to it. Instead, he stared down at her wearing an expression of stone.

At first, he didn't speak. His jaw just flexed like he wasn't sure what to say. But then he opened his mouth, his eyes darkening as he did. "Your part of the bargain is finished." He gestured toward her wrist where the ward from Plumia rested. "You have protection against fae enchantments now. You do not ever have to see me again."

He pointed down a path that led to a beautiful thicket of gold and emerald trees with purple jeweled flowers, a path that led *away* from the pixies' tree. "Go on. Crystalfall will give you everything you need."

Without another word, he spun on his heel and marched off in the opposite direction.

After catching her breath, she called after him. "Revyn, wait."

His step faltered, but he didn't stop marching.

She had to jog to catch up to him. "I want to help you. I don't care about the bargain."

When he caught her eye, he sucked in a sharp exhale. Then he immediately turned away from her, clenching his fists at his side. "I am doing this for my brother. He does not deserve to be controlled the way I always have been. The only reason I am helping the pixies is for him. I cannot lose sight of that."

His tone softened right at the end. He turned his head slightly, immediately capturing her gaze and holding it tight. He stared, and something lit up his eyes. Longing? Was it too hopeful of her to believe he might have longed for her? Just a little bit?

But the look vanished as he clenched his jaw and jerked his head away. "I cannot afford any distractions."

Instead of stomping away this time, he ran. He must have had some fae magic that propelled him forward because he ran faster than any mortal ever could. She tried running after him, but he was completely out of sight before she had taken a few steps.

Her momentum died as her heart twisted into a knot. He had left her.

She reached her arms over her stomach, trying to calm the whirlwind inside. When that did nothing, she hunched her shoulders forward and thought about curling into a ball right there.

How could he just *leave* her? She wanted to help him, and instead, he left her totally defenseless and all alone in a dangerous realm with only a ward bracelet to protect her.

From behind her, the sound of little bells jingled. Plumia.

A rush of relief filled her chest as Clara turned to face the flying pixie.

Rolling her eyes, Plumia scoffed loudly. "And he calls us the dramatic ones." She shrugged slightly. "In his defense, his brother is quite lovely, if a bit grumpy on occasion. I met him once, though I had to fly all the way to Fairfrost to do so. His brother is not quite an adult yet, but he is very close."

She tapped her chin as she flew toward the same path Revyn had taken. "I have to say, I would not mind if Revyn's brother became king of Crystalfall once he gets his magic. He may be from Fairfrost, but I am sure he could do great things for my court if given the chance."

"Plumia." Clara took a small breath. "Do you know how to get back to your tree from here?"

She flew a little higher and tilted her nose upward. "Of course I know. And do not worry, my dear. Bargain or no bargain, you are welcome to help as long as you like. I am certain once we get the tree branches back, your gift for puzzles will help us save the tree once and for all."

Clara tried to calm herself as she followed the pixie. So, Revyn wasn't gone for good. He hadn't left her forever, even if he had tried to. She would see him again soon enough.

Once they started down the path, Plumia stared at her with a sidelong glance. "I must ask though, why? Why are you so determined to help us, even when your bargain has been fulfilled?"

Before answering, Clara found a strand of hair to twirl around one finger. "Because Revyn helped me. He allowed me to escape a life I hated. I cannot leave him trapped by a bargain that impedes his own freedom."

The pixie raised an eyebrow. "But you do not have any bargain or vow or favor or anything with him. What requires you to help him?"

"Honor." Clara let out a long exhale. "Maybe you fae use bargains and favors to decide what is right and what is wrong, but in the mortal realm, we use honor." She placed a hand over her heart and walked a little slower. "We know what is right and what is wrong because we can feel it inside us."

Plumia had completely stopped with any forward progress. Now her golden wings flapped, keeping her hovering in one spot. "Honor. What an interesting thought. Perhaps a mortal would make a good leader as well, although, that is most certainly impossible. Only high fae can become leaders, otherwise I would have attempted to make my own crown and become queen of Crystalfall myself."

They continued down the path a little ways before Plumia spoke again. "And what about that mortal boy who made a deal with the trolls. Is there honor of some sort that directs his actions?"

Clara scowled at the thought. "That is exactly what makes Fritz so problematic. He knows what is right and what is wrong, yet he constantly ignores that knowledge. Everything he does is to help himself and nothing more."

Nodding, Plumia said, "I wonder then why he helped those trolls steal our tree branches. How could it help him to hurt us?"

It was a valid question, but Clara chose to ignore it for the time being. Right now, she only cared about finding the tree and attempting to save as much of it as possible. Once that was done, then she'd work with Revyn to get the missing branches back.

But once Clara and Plumia finally made it back to the tree, they had a much bigger problem to deal with.

A swirling tunnel opened at the top of the hill, only giving Plumia a moment to tug Clara behind the nearest golden tree to hide behind. Peeking around the edge of the trunk, Clara could see who stepped through the door into Crystalfall.

Light blue and silver brocade formed the jacket and pants of the fae, but this jacket and pants looked nothing like the soldier uniform Revyn wore. Instead, it had a fanciful air with lace at the end of the sleeves and at the collar. The fae wearing the clothes had light brown hair and a glare that could probably freeze a lake.

"Revyn." The fae said his name like a curse. "Why have you not returned to Fairfrost yet? You have duties to perform there."

At the bottom of the hill, right next to the pixies' tree, Revyn froze. He turned slowly and immediately nodded. "My king, I will return at once."

He lifted his hand, as if about to open his own Faerie door, but King Pavel just shook his head. "Do not bother with that. Come back with me through my door. I have a job that requires your skills. Some strange mortal managed to get my crown back from those nasty trolls and then the mortal asked for a gem so that he might signal me later. I want my best soldiers with me if the mortal attempts to contact me again."

Clara raised an eyebrow at the words. The only mortal who could possibly have gotten King Pavel's crown was Fritz. Apparently, he had also been busy since coming to Faerie. What other problems would he create while here?

From her hiding spot behind the golden tree, Clara could see how Revyn's shoulders slumped at the king's request. He trudged up the hill, looking more dejected with each step.

"This is a problem," Plumia whispered. "Once Revyn leaves Crystalfall, Faerie itself will compel him to finish his bargain with us. He will be tortured every moment he is in Fairfrost. But King Pavel's magic will keep Revyn stuck in Fairfrost. After being called back like this, it will be nearly impossible for him to get away again. And because of the way our bargain is worded, he cannot use the escape we told him about until after our tree is saved."

The words were ominous of course, but once Revyn and the Fairfrost king disappeared through the door, Clara couldn't help wondering about something else entirely. "*That* was King Pavel? That was the dangerous king of Fairfrost?"

Plumia narrowed her eyes, as if trying to understand. "Yes."

Clara shook her head. "But he's so young. He looks only a year or two older than me, the same age as Revyn. The same age as High Queen Winola. In fact, that mortal man in the throne room of the high court is the oldest person I've seen ever since I got here. Are all fae the same age?"

Placing both hands over her mouth, Plumia snickered. The snickering continued long enough to send heat into Clara's cheeks. After the lengthy chorus of laughter, Plumia finally spoke again. "Oh, my dear, sweet mortal. We are not young, we are immortal. Once fae become adults, our appearance no longer changes."

Clara's head cocked to the side. "So you *are* all the same age? Except for the children? You grow until you become an adult and then you just stop forever?"

Now Plumia's eyebrow rose. "I said our appearance no longer changes, but we do continue to grow. Age is not measured by appearance like it is in the mortal realm. Here in Faerie, age is measured by experience. High Queen Winola is the most experienced being in all of Faerie. A few of the brownies and trolls may have been here longer than her, but no one has as much experience as she does. King Pavel is young compared to her, but he is still older than Revyn."

Plumia narrowed one eye. "Revyn is probably very close to you in age. Though if you stay in Faerie, you will age like a mortal, and he will always appear as he does now. Eventually, you will die once your regular mortal life has been lived. And Revyn, of course, will continue to live forever."

The words wriggled under Clara's skin. Whether the pixie meant to call attention to it or not, Clara suddenly realized a simple kiss with Revyn would never be simple at all. He would live forever. She would age and die.

Before running away, he said he couldn't afford any distractions. Now she realized how much that truly meant. His brother would live forever just like Revyn would. If he ever had to choose between Clara and his brother… Well, she could see now why he resisted any closeness with her. She was just a mortal after all.

The thought sent a sinking feeling through her gut, but it didn't change anything. She was still as determined as ever to save that pixie tree. And even if her future didn't include living out the rest of her days with Revyn, he still deserved the same freedom he had helped her achieve.

She could still help.

But maybe she didn't have to be with him to do it. With a swift head jerk, she turned to look at Plumia. "Can you open one of those Faerie doors too?"

Plumia nodded. "Yes, all fae creatures can, except sprites, but they can fly so fast they have no need for doors."

"Good." Clara stood a little taller. "I need to quickly draw a picture and then we need to find the trolls and steal back your branches. Once we have them, we can figure out a way to get Revyn back here to finish saving the tree."

14

THE PIXIES MADE CLARA A thick fur-lined cloak before they traveled to Fairfrost. Once she stepped foot in the court, she could tell why. A frosty white landscape sat before her, though the snow looked more iridescent than plain white.

Clouds with the same magical iridescence hung in the sky. The land smelled wet, and the air was quiet. Clara stood still while Plumia scanned the area around them.

The pixie had chosen five other pixies to join them. Once Plumia looked around for a bit, she gestured down a hill. Since pixie wings gave off the sound of bells and wind chimes, Clara had to carry all of them as she trudged through the snow and down toward the caverns where the trolls were living.

Water filled with glittering icicles sat the bottom of the hill. The stream was wide, but it only appeared to be a few inches deep. Chunks of ice and large broken boulders sat throughout the stream. The water flowed through it at a slow but steady pace.

Clara had to walk at a strange angle to keep from falling into the stream. At least she could see the entrance to the caverns. Plumia said all the trolls would be sleeping during the day. Sunlight could turn them to stone, so they'd all be hidden at the back of the caverns, sleeping in the shadows.

Snow poured over the golden slippers Clara wore, but magic kept her feet warm and dry anyway. Sneaking up to the cavern entrance, she stayed to the side to assess the situation. Three pixies sat on her shoulders and two sat in her hands. The last pixie, Plumia, sat directly on Clara's head. The pixies didn't weigh much, especially since they were only eight to ten inches tall, but Clara was still grateful when they offered to sit on a nearby rock.

She carefully helped them onto the boulder so they wouldn't have to use their wings, and then she took her first glance inside the cavern.

Just as Plumia had promised, the green trolls slept at the very back of the cavern, well within the shadows. The golden tree branches from the pixies sat at the front. Revyn had claimed the trolls would fight anyone who entered, but how much could they do while asleep?

If Clara had the strength of a fae, she would have marched forward and gathered all the missing tree branches right then and there. But even without massive strength, they still had one last problem.

Fritz sat close to the front of the cavern, warming his hands by a small fire. He hadn't noticed Clara yet, but if she moved any closer to the tree branches, he would.

He sat next to a shallow puddle of water that held a creature that was woman on top and fish on bottom. A mermaid. The creature had dark skin and big purple and brown eyes. Her tail was shimmery purple and silver, which matched her purple and silver hair.

It seemed cruel to only allow her a tiny puddle to sit in. It barely even covered her tail. Even worse, her body was clearly not accustomed to the climate of Fairfrost. She was shivering and gasping for air. Her purple and silver hair looked natural, but the blue tinge on her dark lips did not.

"Aren't you finished yet?" Fritz snapped at the mermaid.

Her entire body shuddered as she stirred something inside a small cauldron over the fire. "It t-t-takes longer to boil when the air is so c-cold."

Her teeth chattered even after she finished speaking. The sight of the mermaid freezing while Fritz complained about food lit a fire of determination inside Clara.

She scanned the cavern, looking carefully at strategic points. The stone walls had suitable footholds so she'd be able to climb it like she had hoped. She'd have to be slow and completely silent though if she had any chance of completing her task without alerting Fritz.

It wasn't ideal, but it would work. Hopefully.

Clara turned now to Plumia and nodded. Since they had discussed the plan ahead of time, Plumia already knew what to do. She and the other pixies waved their hands and started conjuring a heavy rope made of gold.

Taking one end of it, Clara hiked up her skirt and began climbing the wall of the cavern. Now she could only hope that whatever the mermaid stirred over the fire would be enough to keep her and Fritz busy enough that they wouldn't notice Clara.

Luckily, her golden slippers didn't just press against the stone wall. Somehow, the magical footwear seemed to grip onto it, giving Clara steady footing no matter how high she climbed.

She took a deep, satisfied breath now that the plan had started. Most people never thought to look up, so hiding would be much easier if she did it from above.

With the golden rope in her hand, Clara trekked across the cavern wall until she reached the point where the shadows began. From there, she pulled one of the metal pins the pixies had previously prepared for her and used it to pin the golden rope in place.

As she made her trek back to the cavern entrance, Fritz spat liquid from his mouth. "This is what you eat? This is the most disgusting thing I've ever tasted in my life."

The mermaid ran her hands up and down her arms as her whole body shivered. "This is what the trolls eat. They have not allowed me any other food since they captured me. I have nothing else to cook."

Fritz knocked the bowl over, and the liquid splashed against a cavern wall. "I'm not eating that filth. You should be ashamed you served it to me."

The blue tinge in the mermaid's lips turned an even brighter blue as she breathed out a foggy breath. "Let me tell a story."

Clara had reached the spot where she pinned the first bit of golden rope into place. With the new rope in hand, she now tied it to the first and then pinned it a little farther down the wall.

As she started climbing back, slowly, she managed to catch a glimpse of Fritz's scowl.

"What?" he asked

"A story," the mermaid repeated. "Let me tell a story. It will give me strength."

His nose wrinkled. "Will it help you cook better?"

The mermaid rocked her body back and forth, shivering harder than ever. "M-maybe."

Fritz rolled his eyes. "Fine, then make it quick."

The mermaid began her tale with her hands still rubbing the goose bumps that covered her arms. "Magic began in the first realm, the mortal realm. The first fae, Nouvel, roamed the world alongside the mortals. He had great magic, magic so powerful the mortals began to fear him."

As Clara slowly, carefully made her way across the cavern wall with a new golden rope, she saw the exact moment Fritz changed from annoyed to interested. The moment the mermaid mentioned power, his eyes lit up. He sat a little taller and looked more carefully at the mermaid.

"Magic in the mortal realm?" He raised both eyebrows. "I did not know that was possible."

The blue tinge in the mermaid's lips had softened to an almost pink color now. Her hand still rubbed over her arms, but goose bumps no longer covered them. "As the mortals grew more fearful of Nouvel, they also grew more violent. They sought to kill the first fae. Seeing that he had no other choice, Nouvel ripped a tear in the fabric of space and created a new realm, the realm of Faerie."

Though he had been leaning forward, Fritz shook his head and sat back again. "Is this story almost over?"

Clara had pinned five golden ropes to the ceiling now. With them in place, she started twisting and knotting them together.

Letting out a long breath, the mermaid finally dropped her hands onto her scaly lap. This breath didn't appear as foggy as the others had. "After using so much magic to create the realm, Nouvel began breaking apart. He could not stay in his original form, so he formed new fae, smaller fae, from the different parts of his body. The high fae came from his head. The mermaids came from his tongue. Dryads came from his fingernails. When all the new fae had been formed, all that remained of him became a bundle of creation magic, which still sits at the center of Faerie."

Fritz had started tapping his shoe against the ground, but it stopped suddenly. His entire body went completely still for several seconds. After another moment, he sucked in a breath and turned slowly toward the mermaid. "A bundle of creation magic?"

His eyes practically glowed with greed.

The mermaid's shoulders relaxed as she leaned backward. "The fae cannot touch the creation magic. If we touch it, our magic is sucked back into the bundle."

Fritz leaned so far forward, he nearly lost his balance. "But that's only because you have magic to begin with, right? If a mortal touched the creation magic..."

He left the sentence open, waiting for the mermaid to finish it.

She shrugged. "I suppose that mortal would be given magic of his own."

A conniving smile twitched at the corners of Fritz's mouth. "Magic of his own."

He reached for the nearest golden tree branch, which was slightly curved. With it in his hands, he grabbed another small tree branch and twisted it around the first. After the third tree branch, his intention became clear. He was forming a crown.

After managing a basic circlet shape, he grabbed emerald leaves and crammed them into the twisted branches. The attempts to create tines were crude, but they worked. If making a crown was all it took to become the leader of a court, Clara was quickly running out of time to stop him.

Her fingers flew across the golden rope on the ceiling, desperate to finish the net she had been twisting and tying. She knew it would be impossible to fight the trolls on her own, but if she could trap them under a heavy golden net, then hopefully she could steal the tree branches while they were stuck.

She had thought of the idea after she and Revyn got stuck in a net themselves, only this net would come from above instead of below.

Fritz started tapping his toe again, but it only served to increase the greed in his eyes. "Where is the creation magic?"

"At the center of Faerie." The mermaid looked more relaxed with each detail she added to the story. Her body no longer shivered.

Fritz nodded. "Which court?"

She shrugged. "The high court, I guess. I have never seen the creation magic, but many say you can see it in High Queen Winola's eyes. I assume the magic must be close to her, especially since she rules the high court."

He stood up with a start, moving toward the back of the cavern. I need to wake the trolls immediately, before it gets dark. I want them vulnerable when I show them the crown."

After kicking one of the trolls in the side, the creature groaned and opened its eyes.

Clara hadn't had any trouble hiding from Fritz near the top of the cavern. But the trolls all lay on the stone floor with their eyes pointed upward. When Fritz kicked the creature awake, her hiding form was the first thing it saw.

The troll sat up and growled, which startled awake a few of the other trolls. It lifted an enormous stone-like finger at her and said a single word. "Mortal."

Pain twisted in her chest while a flood of electricity seemed to shoot through her veins. She needed to get out of there. Now.

Fritz turned his gaze upward. When he caught sight of Clara and her makeshift net across the ceiling, he just chuckled.

"Well, who knew I would get another chance to ruin your life? Don't you worry, my dearest betrothed, I won't fail at it this time."

Before she could even think of scrambling across the wall and back to the entrance of the cave, Fritz produced a shimmering blue crystal from his pocket, which he immediately crushed in his fist.

The moment his hand closed over the crystal, a bright light filled the entire cavern. Within another breath, a swirling Faerie door appeared near the entrance of the cavern.

Her heart stuttered. Her fingers shook, nearly losing her grip on the wall. More fae would soon walk through that door and into the cavern. The trolls looked as surprised about it as she did.

But surprised or not, one thing was clear. No one would be able to stop the fae from arriving. And judging by the look on Fritz's face, their arrival would be anything but good.

15

Her heart may have been racing so fast she could barely breathe, but that wouldn't stop Clara from trying to reach the mouth of the cave. Once she got to the exit, she could pull on the golden rope, which would drop the net she had just twisted and tied to the top of the cavern.

The trolls would be trapped underneath it. Fritz would be trapped underneath it.

Clara would have just enough time to jump away before the metal rope fell. She and the pixies had planned this all before they ever got to Fairfrost, except the trolls were supposed to be asleep.

After Fritz had kicked them awake, they growled and spat and threw rocks to make her lose her grip on the wall. In the end, Fritz was the one who pulled her down. He grabbed onto her ankle and yanked so hard her head snapped back. She tried to hold on with her fingers, but the quick movement and sharp stone left scratches on her fingertips that brought a few drops of blood.

She expected to land on the stone floor of the cavern, and possibly even injure her ankles. She expected Fritz to slap her or kick her or maybe even stab her. The wild look in his eyes proved him capable of it.

But before her body touched the ground, another figure in the room rushed forward and caught her in his arms. She had to blink before she recognized Revyn. Then she had to blink again while trying to figure out where he had come from. Was this a dream?

It only took another moment to piece together what had happened. A Faerie door had appeared in the cavern just before Fritz yanked Clara down from the wall. She had momentarily forgotten about it, but she could see now that Revyn had come through the door along with King Pavel and three other soldiers.

The fae clearly had speed mortals did not because no mortal could have rushed forward quickly enough to save Clara from her fall. Revyn even sneered at Fritz when the mortal young man tried to come closer to Clara.

"Who is that?" King Pavel stared with an open mouth at Clara and then at Revyn, who held her safely in his arms.

Shaking his head, the king now turned to Fritz. "I got your signal, but I do not understand why you called me to a trolls' cavern, especially one where the trolls are awake."

Each of the trolls took that as a sign to start growling, which sounded like rocks grinding across glass and steel.

The king glared at them. "Be careful. You know I have magic too great for you to defeat."

That didn't stop the trolls from growling, but they lowered the volume of it slightly. Now the king pinched the bridge of his nose. "Put her down, Revyn. I still do not understand why she is here." Once again, his gaze pinned on Fritz. "What is going on here, mortal?"

Revyn did lower Clara to the ground. He held her carefully until certain she was balanced and steady before he pulled his arms away from her. Even then, he took a pointed glance into her eyes, as if trying to communicate something.

Considering how he had abruptly abandoned her the last time they had been together, she liked to think he was trying to apologize. More than likely, he just wanted to figure out how and *why* she was in that cavern, but she much preferred the apology theory.

Being so busy making up apologies for Revyn, she almost didn't see the twisted grimace on Fritz's face as he stood a little taller. "Do not call me *mortal.* You should call me…"

His voice trailed off suddenly as he stared at the snowy white landscape outside the cavern. "You know, I never liked the name Fritz. Maybe I should choose a new name for myself now that I'm in a different realm. Call me Metternich." He waved his hand through the air. "No, I deserve better than my father's surname. Call me—"

"Why am I here?" King Pavel practically roared the question, shaking the entire cavern. A few glittering icicles dropped from the ceiling, smashing into iridescent clouds.

"Oh, right. That." Fritz turned back toward the trolls, who all stared at him with heads tilted to the side. "I made a bargain with the trolls, but I figured, why not betray them and make a deal with you instead?"

The trolls kept their heads tilted for two seconds longer before the words sank in. But then, all at once, their eyes widened, and their stone-like fingers clenched into fists. "Betrayer!" they shouted, almost in unison.

But each troll only managed a single step forward before Fritz raised one finger. "Ah," he said in an eerily calm voice. "If you try to come after me, I'll just run into the sunlight. If you follow, you'll be turned to stone."

King Pavel lifted his eyebrows, clearly impressed…until Fritz turned to him.

Now the look in Fritz's eye promised another trick. "And if you, King of Fairfrost, try to hurt me, I'll just give the trolls what they want and let them destroy you."

The king had made a show before of not fearing the trolls, but this declaration caused him to clear his throat and glance around anxiously. He took a small step back, then immediately tried to play it off like he was simply adjusting his feet. But the fact that he tried to hide his fear only served to make him appear more fearful than before.

The soldiers he had brought with him took a few steps backward as well. All except Revyn. He stood still as he narrowed his eyes at the others. He had set Clara down like the king ordered, but he hadn't moved away from her. One arm at his side even twitched, as if ready to throw it in front of her if any danger came her way.

The whole situation was completely preposterous. Fritz thoroughly controlled the room, even though he didn't have a single person on his side. The trolls were afraid of turning to stone in the sunlight. The king and the Fairfrost soldiers were afraid of being attacked by the trolls. Yet both sides failed to realize they could simply turn on their common enemy, Fritz, and the entire thing would be over at once.

"Before we start negotiating, I offer this mortal to you as a slave for your household." Fritz gestured toward Clara, wearing a smirk that chilled her to the bone.

She had to take a breath before she could scoff, which honestly ruined the whole effect of the scoff. There was no point in trying to save face now. "Um, no."

Fritz's nostrils flared. "I'm in charge here, and I have decided you would make a lovely present for the ruler of Fairfrost. King Pavel, wouldn't you like her?"

The king's eyes flashed with a greed even worse than Fritz's. He ogled over Clara's entire form. "I could always add another consort to my harem."

"My king." Revyn spoke suddenly, possibly even before he had decided what to say. He had also taken a step forward, slightly in front of Clara. But now that the king stared at him, he didn't seem sure of what to say next. After clearing his throat, he continued. "I am certain the mother of your child does not want you to have another consort."

King Pavel raised an eyebrow. "Yes, but she is not the leader of Fairfrost. I am. That means I can choose as many consorts as I like." His mouth lifted into a sickly grin. "Besides, her jealousy fuels me, and this one," he pointed at Clara, "would make her rage."

Clara's gut knotted and bile shot up her throat. Back home, she never would have stood up for herself in a situation like this, but she was in Faerie now. Curling her hands into fists, she took a step forward. "You're not taking me as a consort. You wouldn't want me anyway." Her chin tilted up. "If you tried to take me, I would stab you in your sleep during my first night in your castle."

The king gulped, and he even took another step back. He may have acted powerful, but this king clearly relied on fear to get respect, instead of relying on any actual ability.

Fritz rolled his eyes. "Fine, I'll just kill her myself later. But first, let's get to the negotiations." He retrieved the gold and emerald makeshift crown that had been hiding under his jacket. He lifted it high for the king and all the trolls to see. "I have a crown made of tree branches from Crystalfall. That's right. A *crown*."

As Fritz continued to lay out his terms, Clara edged back until she stood close enough to Revyn to whisper. "Plumia is just outside the cavern. She can open a door for you and get you back to Crystalfall to save the tree."

Revyn's eyes glinted. He gave her that same look of awe that somehow made her feel like she could soar. "You are cleverer than I expected." He lowered his voice even more. "But it does not matter if I go through Plumia's door. King Pavel will still know where to find me."

By now, Fritz had told the Fairfrost king and the trolls that whichever of them made the better offer would get the crown. King Pavel started the bidding by offering a large estate with brownies to cook and clean and dozens of other servants to do the rest.

While the king spoke, Clara used her chin to point to the cavern entrance. She then nudged Revyn with her elbow, and they both started inching toward the opening. Only then did she start whispering again. "I drew a picture in the soil of how I believe the tree is supposed to look. Even though the king knows where to find you, we should be able to save it if we can do it quickly enough."

Her chin now pointed to the pile of tree branches at the very front of the cavern. "How many of those can you carry?"

He threw her a grin filled with arrogance. "All of them." His eyes narrowed as he glanced back at the king and the three other soldiers that came with them. "I will need a moment to gather the branches though."

Since they had nearly reached the entrance to the cavern, Clara threw her own confident grin. "Oh, I can give you time."

With a yank, she then pulled on the golden rope right next to her. The force of it ripped the net from the pins that had held it in place. In a flash, the heavy net dropped down until it covered every person inside the cavern except her and Revyn.

She didn't have to explain how little time they had. He immediately began gathering branches into his arms. They needed the crown, too, the one currently in Fritz's hands. Without all the original pieces of the tree, the tree would never be fully saved. Fritz, the king, the Fairfrost soldiers, and even the trolls all squirmed and shouted at the net trapping them.

Clara had been hoping she'd be able to dash over and pluck the crown right from Fritz's hands once the net fell. Unfortunately, he had the crown pulled tight to his chest with no way for her to reach it.

She glanced back at Revyn and gestured toward the side where Plumia and the other pixies waited. "You go on and start working on the tree. I have to get the crown from Fritz, and then I'll be right there."

Revyn nodded and disappeared out the cavern mouth with bundles of golden tree branches in his arms.

But as Clara rushed toward the net, intending to stay on top of it. One of the trolls roared and managed to stand up straight for a few seconds. The weight of the net, along with some pixie-imbued magic, pulled the troll down to the ground eventually, but by then, the damage had been done.

Clara's foot caught in the net, dragging her to the ground. She still managed to crawl toward Fritz, and even grabbed hold of the crown. When she yanked the crown away, he let it go.

The fact that he released the crown so easily seemed exactly as suspicious as it should have. Once the crown left his hands, he immediately reached out and caught hold of Clara's ankle, twisting her deeper into the net.

King Pavel shouted at his guards. The trolls growled and gnashed their teeth. But Fritz just smiled. He reached out and grabbed the end of the golden net that would free him. He'd be free, and Clara would be stuck.

Her heart leapt into her throat as she searched for a way to fix this. Her eyes scanned the net. She examined the cavern.

And then she saw it.

The size and shapes of every item in the room measured themselves perfectly in her mind. It didn't take any effort at all.

If Clara grabbed another section of the net and pulled it just so, it would cover Fritz, and he would be stuck again. The plan only had one little problem.

If she pulled the net just so, she'd be stuck too.

Fritz must have seen her mind working. He never knew how good she was at estimating sizes and shapes, but he must have seen the look of triumph on her face. He must have known he had one chance to save himself.

He thrust a hand into his pocket and pulled out a piece of paper with a short note written on it. It must have been something he'd written ahead of time, just in case. After placing the note in Clara's free hand, he raised an eyebrow at her. "You aren't going to take that crown back to Crystalfall. That note explains why."

His tone dripped with confidence. He was so certain he would win. Despite her entire past, Clara still looked down at the note. Of course, she couldn't read a single word on it. The letters jumped and danced and refused to stay still. She only processed the look of his handwriting, which seemed cramped and a little too straight.

Maybe in the note he promised her wealth untold if she'd promise in return to let him go. Maybe he swore to end their engagement and just leave her be. Maybe he claimed they could find a way to the creation magic together and both receive magic from Faerie. It didn't matter because she knew who he was. He'd turn on anyone who joined his side the moment it became convenient for him to do so.

But the note made her realize something she'd never been brave enough to admit before. All these years she wanted freedom from her parents, freedom from her miserable life. Maybe all that time she'd been after the wrong thing. She didn't need freedom. She needed to accept who she was. She needed to embrace her strengths instead of always burying them under her weaknesses. She needed to see herself as someone great instead of as someone flawed.

The smile that lifted her lips felt like magic, her own magic. It even made Fritz cower a little, which only lifted her smile even more. "Want to know my secret?" she asked. Crumpling the note in her fist, she chuckled. "I can't read."

With a single throw, the crumpled note fell on the other side of the cavern. It freed her hand, which allowed her to pull the net just so.

The net twisted and shifted, and soon, both she and Fritz, along with the king, soldiers, and trolls, all remained stuck underneath the golden net.

Her other hand still held the crown, but she tossed it close to the cavern entrance. "Plumia!"

The sound of quiet wind chimes jingled right away.

When the sugar pixie appeared at the front of the cavern, Clara pointed at the golden circlet. "Take the crown and then shut your door. You're going to have to save the tree without me."

Plumia's eyes went wide. She stared, realizing the net held Clara down and she couldn't be freed unless all the others were released too. Plumia's face turned ashen, but it didn't stop her from acting.

Nodding at Clara, the pixie swooped down and lifted the crown off the ground. "Your sacrifice will not be forgotten." Plumia then flew awkwardly under the heavy weight of the crown and disappeared around the entrance of the cavern.

The momentary peace that filled Clara's heart quickly fluttered away. Maybe Lifespark Tree would be saved and the pixies would live and Revyn would be free of his bargain, but none of those things changed her current situation.

The golden net still covered her, and everyone else stuck under it with her had good reason to want her dead.

16

Clara had always been good at drawing. She enjoyed it, too, but the shame of not being able to read or write often kept her away from pencils. If she'd been able to accept herself years ago, how would her drawing skills have flourished? How much better would her drawings be today?

The questions plagued her mostly because her drawing had the chance to save the pixies…or end them. To save Revyn…or trap him forever. Now that she was stuck in Fairfrost, under a golden net and deep inside a troll cavern, she couldn't help them save the pixie tree. She could only hope the drawing she had done that showed which branches went where on the tree would be enough that they could save it themselves.

"You can't read?" Fritz had his back against the ground with the heavy golden net pressing down on him, but it didn't stop him from laughing. "That's your secret?" Now he laughed harder.

"Maybe we should try lifting that corner there," King Pavel said to his soldiers. Together, they started lifting a corner of the net.

Everything suddenly seemed to move too fast as dizziness buzzed in Clara's head. Made from gold, the net was much heavier than rope, plus it had magic from the pixies, making it even heavier. But with so many beings underneath the net, it also had far too many beings looking for a way out. Would she be able to stop them long enough to allow Revyn and the pixies save the tree?

Before she could try to sabotage the king's attempt at getting free, Fritz lifted himself onto his elbow and wrinkled his nose at Clara. "Your parents were right to hide your secret. No one ever would have agreed to marry you if they had known. You're a simpleton, a nitwit, an imbecile. Who would ever choose to be with someone so stupid?"

If her parents had been there, they would have been mortified. They might have crawled over to the trolls and begged to be eaten on the spot. They'd have died knowing someone thought of their progeny in such a way. They'd be embarrassed they had created such a flawed and doltish daughter.

But the fire in Clara's heart that had allowed her to crumple that note still burned within her. She didn't even bother looking him in the eye. She just smiled calmly and let the fire flow through her veins. "So what if I can't read? I trapped you under this net, didn't I? You might even say that makes me better than you."

Fritz spat straight in her face. "I am a *thousand* times better than you. How dare a simpleton like you even attempt to speak to me like an equal. You should bow to me."

She stopped listening. Why bother when all he did was spout off nonsense? And besides, both King Pavel and the trolls were getting very close to finding a way out from under the golden net. Clara tugged on different spots, trapping them more completely each time, but she couldn't do this forever. Like it or not, they were going to find a way out.

Now was probably a good time to figure out what to do when that happened.

At that exact moment, she noticed the light changing outside the cavern. Darkness had started closing in. The last tendrils of sunlight were slipping down the horizon.

Her breath caught in her throat as she glanced behind her. Now the trolls would be able to leave the cavern. Even if they gave up on trying to get a crown to rule Crystalfall, they'd still probably want to get back to that tree and destroy it, just for revenge.

At that moment, King Pavel lifted part of the net just enough that Clara could no longer keep him further trapped. He still had to crawl under a few ropes of the golden net, but he would be free soon.

Clara reached for the golden ropes twisted around her ankle. If the king and his soldiers were about to be free, she needed to free herself and fast.

The king muttered under his breath as he moved. "I cannot believe Revyn is trying to escape my court. I should kill those pixies for helping him."

Her gut clenched at those words. Even if Revyn managed to save the tree, he still needed to escape from Fairfrost with his younger brother. If the king was angry with Revyn for trying to escape, he might keep Revyn closer than ever. He might even throw Revyn into a dungeon.

There had to be a way to help. Clara gulped. Her fingers kept trying to free her ankle from the net, but now she sat forward and made eye contact with the Fairfrost king. "That's not why Revyn is helping the pixies. He's not trying to escape your court. It's just that, uh, the pixies," her head tilted to the side until an idea came to her, "enchanted him. The pixies enchanted him and forced him to help until their tree is saved."

King Pavel immediately stopped crawling and stared straight at her. "They did?"

It seemed a miracle that he believed her, especially when she hadn't been all that convincing. But if it this was working, she was happy to go with it. "Oh, yes. It's all true."

The king shook his head a little before going back to crawling again. "He is very simple minded if he fell under the enchantment of a pixie. Perhaps he should not serve in the castle guard. I may have to demote him to one of the outer cities."

Clara's fingers tugged at the ropes on her ankle, barely loosening the tightest one. Her heart skipped at the king's suggestion. If Revyn was relegated to an outer city, surely, that would make it more difficult for the king to check up on him. The king might not ever notice when Revyn escaped the court with his younger brother. She tried not to sound too hopeful when she responded. "I agree. I'm sure a simple-minded soldier like him would be much better served in one of the outer cities."

"She's lying." Fritz held a hand outward, shaking his head in disbelief. "She's obviously lying."

"Lying." King Pavel scoffed. "That is impossible. We may be able to deceive, but no one can speak an outright lie. I do wonder when the pixies enchanted him. I suppose it must have happened after the trolls stole my crown."

Despite the conflict between them, Clara and Fritz glanced toward each other. The realization in his face probably matched that in hers. If what King Pavel said was true, then that meant…fae could not lie. Could that possibly be true?

The realization in Fritz's face immediately changed to scheming. He turned to the king with a wide smile. "I have a way to get your Crystalfall crown back. I just need you to show me where the creation magic is."

King Pavel had almost reached the end of the net. His three soldiers crawled just behind him. At Fritz's words, the king glanced back. "The creation magic that the first fae left behind? Why would you want to go near that? It takes away fae magic if we touch it."

For the second time in only a few sentences, the king assumed mortals were the same as fae. But if the mermaid trapped inside the cavern was right, then the creation magic would not affect a mortal in the same way at all. If that were true, Fritz would have the ambition of a mortal with the magic of a fae. A doomed combination if there ever was one.

Fritz got onto his hands and knees and started finding his own way out from under the net. All the trolls did the same. Fritz huffed. "I know what happens at the creation magic. It doesn't matter why I want to go there. I just do. Don't you want your crown back? Show me where the creation magic is, and I can help with that."

Clara could more easily tell which areas of the net to crawl toward thanks to her gift of seeing measurements. She managed to find a way out from under the net at nearly the same moment King Pavel did. The Fairfrost king crawled out, stretching out his legs as he stood. "If you want to join me, you will help me find the crown before anything else. Then we can worry about the creation magic."

Fritz huffed again. "Fine. We can get the crown first, but then I need you to show me where the magic is hidden."

King Pavel, his soldiers, and even Fritz weren't that aggressive when they emerged from the golden net. The king clearly wanted the crown so he could rule Crystalfall, but he and the others didn't seem eager to rip Clara to shreds like she first thought they might.

Everything changed when the trolls finally threw off the net. They ground their teeth together, making little particles crumble from their mouths, as if their teeth were truly rocks that they ground to dust.

The nearest troll swiped a fist straight at Clara's gut. It only missed because she leapt toward the wall of the cave and the magic in her shoes helped her to stick to it.

Another troll with yellow eyes hissed as it pointed at Clara. "Kill it."

She would have run outside the cave and into the light, except the light had disappeared. Night had fallen, which gave her no protection against the trolls.

King Pavel wrinkled his nose at the trolls lumbering toward the front of the cave. With a wave of his hand, he opened a Faerie door, probably headed for the pixie's tree, and casually stepped into it. His soldiers and Fritz followed after him.

With another troll ready to slam a fist into her gut, Clara realized she had exactly one option. Jump inside that door and hope against all hope it would still be open when she got to it.

17

WITH EYES SLAMMED SHUT, CLARA couldn't tell what surface her body landed against. Was it the black pebbled soil of Crystalfall? Or had she missed the door and landed on the stone cavern with the trolls behind her? One peek through her eyelids would provide the answer, but a rock-hard sensation in her belly made her too afraid to try.

"Clara."

The sound of Revyn's voice sent a rush of relief through her. She had made it to Crystalfall. When she finally dared open her eyes, he had already dropped to his knees in front of her.

She had to arch her back slightly to see past him to the center of the valley. The tree looked decent. Many of the branches had already been attached correctly. Apparently, her drawing had been good enough after all. Only about half of the branches remained.

After her examination, she finally turned her gaze back to Revyn. He performed an examination of his own, searching her arms and face and side. His brow furrowed as he searched. She couldn't imagine why he looked at her so intently or what he could be searching for. Unless he was searching for injuries.

One corner of her mouth lifted. "Were you worried about me?"

"Yes." Revyn answered without hesitation. "Plumia would not tell me what happened to you."

His arms opened almost like he intended to wrap her up in them. At the last moment, he lifted one hand instead, brushing a thumb across her cheek. "I am glad to see you well."

At the mention of Plumia, Clara glanced across the valley to search for the little pixie. She found the creature sitting on a rock, except something about her looked duller than usual.

At that moment, the tree's golden hue darkened to a wooden brown. The pulse only lasted a split second, but when the tree returned to its usual color, the gold looked significantly less brilliant than before.

Gathering her velvety pink skirt in one hand, Clara got to her feet and started toward the tree. They still had a lot of work to do.

Revyn reached for a nearby branch. "I was going to attach this one next, right in this spot."

He didn't ask a question, but the way he looked at her still made the inquiry clear. Even though several of the branches had been attached correctly, he clearly still trusted her to choose the right spot better than him.

With a swift nod, she glanced at the tree and then at the branch. Her gaze turned back to the tree again. "Maybe try that spot, just a little lower."

By the time she finished speaking, he already had the branch against the tree in exactly the spot she pointed out. When he melted it against the tree with his magic, it attached perfectly as golden as the trunk without any line of brown running through it.

Neither of them could enjoy the victory though because Fritz huffed loudly behind them. "Where is the crown?"

Revyn tugged Clara a little closer to himself and then he glared at Fritz. "You think I left it as a crown?" He gestured upward to the golden branches with glittering emerald leaves. "The pieces are back up there where they should be. Only Faerie itself can choose the ruler of this court. I would not look to defy Faerie if I were you."

When he finished speaking, King Pavel stepped out from the other side of the golden tree with his three soldiers behind him.

Revyn took a step back and stared wide-eyed. He must have been so distracted by the tree that he hadn't noticed anyone step through the door until Clara had come hurtling through it.

The king tilted his head to the side. "And what about me? Do you think I am wrong for trying to become leader of this land?"

Clara donned her sweetest smile and edged her shoulder in front of Revyn's chest slightly. "It's just the enchantment. He cannot help it. He cannot do anything except save the tree."

Revyn's eyes narrowed as he turned toward her. "What en—"

She grabbed his hand and pulled him away from the king and the other soldiers. "Come on, Revyn. I tried to keep them back as long as possible, but the trolls will be here soon. They are not very happy with me for trapping them under that net."

Revyn kept trying to catch her gaze, probably wondering about the enchantment she had mentioned. Since the king hadn't known it, Revyn probably didn't understand mortals could lie. That would take more time to explain than they had. They needed to focus on the tree.

As they moved toward the next tree branch, Revyn looked up at the sky and scowled. "I did not realize night had fallen already. The trolls will be able to leave their cavern."

"Here, try this branch next." Clara gestured toward the longest branch still sitting on the black soil. "I'm almost certain it goes right above that branch we just attached."

While they moved, the king threw a glare at Fritz. "And where is my crown?"

Fritz stared open-mouthed at him before throwing his hands into the air. "Is every fae stupid? You could make a crown out of anything, out of the grass even. Why am I the only one who has even tried?"

He started up the hill, heading straight for the strands of green pearls that formed the grass. Clara was almost certain they did not want Fritz to finish his crown, but right now, saving the tree had to be the highest priority.

King Pavel seemed vaguely interested in Fritz's claim that he could make a crown from the grass, but judging by the fact that he did not follow Fritz, the king clearly held little belief it could actually be done. Instead of following, the king settled into a spot at the edge of the valley with his other soldiers standing behind him. "Since the pixies enchanted you, Revyn, I will wait until you are finished with the tree and then we can go back to Fairfrost."

Revyn pressed his eyebrows together, trying to understand the king's words. Before he could say anything to give away Clara's lie, she pushed him back toward the tree. "Don't worry about him. Let's get back to work."

Luckily, Revyn's bargain compelled him strongly enough that he seemed to forget all about the king. Immediately, his focus turned back to the tree and the branches. He finally lifted the branch Clara had pointed out earlier.

That second branch did not attach perfectly on the first try, but after adjusting it slightly higher on the trunk, they finally got it to attach without a line of brown inside it.

Biting her lip, Clara glanced back at Plumia.

The pixie slumped on her rock. Her wings wilted and looked decidedly less shimmery than they had in Fairfrost.

"Are you almost finished?" Even Plumia's voice sounded wispy and tired compared to earlier.

Clara gulped at the sound of it. She pointed out another branch, which Revyn lifted right away. But by the time he held it against the tree, Plumia's wings sagged even more.

"Right there." Clara picked at the collar of her dress as she waited for Revyn's magic to attach the branch. It was getting easier now that only a few open spots remained, but they still had several branches left.

The golden branch attached perfectly, but almost immediately afterward, the entire tree pulsed brown and wooden. It took three whole seconds before it changed back to gold. Even then, the gold appeared duller than ever.

Sucking in a sharp inhale, Clara turned to Revyn. "We need to hurry."

He didn't have time to offer a response. Before he could, a chorus of growls and gurgles erupted from the top of the hill.

The trolls had arrived.

18

CLARA SET HER FEET SHOULDER width apart atop the black soil of Crystalfall. She slowed her breath until it came out steady and sure. Maybe she'd never been in a fight before meeting Revyn, but she had spent years enduring shouts and screams and baseless accusations. She didn't know how to wield an axe, but if she had learned anything since coming to Faerie, she knew how to stand her ground.

The trolls stood at the top of the hill, their green skin clear even in the dusky light. They gurgled and shouted words that sounded more like coughs. Their fists clenched and they bared their rock-like teeth.

But when they began to charge forward, they didn't move in the direction Clara expected. Her stomach flopped over on itself as the trolls began running. They didn't come down the hill. They didn't come toward Clara or the tree or any of the sprites.

Instead, they ran toward Fritz.

Her mouth twisted up in the lightest smile. Of course they would be angry at him. She should have realized that. After all, he had blatantly betrayed them when asking for a better offer from King Pavel. Maybe the trolls wouldn't be an issue.

She spun on her heel and immediately moved toward the next tree branch she wanted to attach. Revyn stood with an open mouth, staring at the trolls. After she caught his attention, he shook his head and grabbed a golden branch. She pointed out where it and the next two tree branches belonged.

They only had a dozen left to attach, which made it even easier to see where the pieces went.

"Kill it!" the trolls shouted, nearly to Fritz's location now.

Fritz dropped the partially-finished crown made of grassy strands of green pearls. He took a step back.

In that moment, a new fear took hold of Clara, one that twisted deeper than seeing those trolls at the top of the hill. It was such a subtle thing, but she had learned by now to fear it more than anything else.

Maybe Fritz was frightened, but he also had a look of scheming on his face. For all his faults, no one could think as quickly as him. No one could turn things in his favor with only a handful of words.

Just before the trolls reached him, the fear on Fritz's face turned to one of confusion. His entire body slouched as if he were as relaxed as a sleepy man sitting next to a cozy fire.

The change in his demeanor was enough to make a few of the trolls stumble. That couldn't be good.

Fritz shrugged with complete confusion and utter relaxation. "What are you doing?" he asked the trolls.

The words ripped the fight out of them just long enough for the trolls to stop running. They stumbled to a stop. It only took a breath before their shock wore off. The troll at the front of the group lifted a finger and jammed it toward Fritz. "You betrayer. You die."

But Fritz shook his head and pinched the bridge of his nose. "No, no, no. You don't want to kill me. You want to kill *her*." He gestured down the hill and straight at Clara. "She's the one who trapped you under that golden net, which probably would have crushed you if you hadn't escaped. She's the one who killed your troll king."

The trolls blinked their big eyes, unclenching their fists as they tilted their heads to the side.

Fritz stood taller now. A smirk even formed on his mouth. "And you hate the pixies, too, for how they tried to hurt you last time you were here. Remember how they threw gems into your eyes?"

The trolls started nodding.

Clara gulped, but she didn't have time to waste worrying about the trolls. They'd be charging down that hill soon enough, which meant they needed to get the rest of the branches onto the tree as quickly as possible.

"Get that one there." She gestured at a tree branch across the valley and then rushed to the one closest to her.

Revyn still stared at the trolls.

"Revyn, get the branch."

When he finally tore his gaze away, his posture was as wilted as the features on his face. "You are in danger."

"Yes, and standing here isn't going to change that. Now grab that branch, so we can save this tree. We only have a few moments before we have to deal with those trolls."

A swarm of pixies suddenly arrived. Their little chiming wings sounded more like broken glass when they flew. The creatures didn't even seem to notice the trolls. The pixies just flew down to where Plumia slumped and then they all slumped on the rocks and ground around her.

The tree pulsed brown. Each of the pixies groaned and held their stomachs as if they could feel the pain of the tree right inside them.

Fritz stood taller than ever. Fire had entered his tone, fire that fueled the trolls. Fritz practically shouted now. "You only want two things: to destroy that tree, and to destroy that girl."

That one last cry roused the trolls into action. They roared and charged down the hill louder than ever.

Clara had a heavy golden branch in her hands. She dragged it toward the tree as well as she could. She wasn't much use with her mortal strength. At least Revyn had managed to attach another two branches before the trolls made it to the valley.

Once they got to the bottom, Revyn rushed forward until he positioned himself directly in front of Clara. She pushed him away at once.

"Don't worry about me. Just focus on saving that tree."

He looked about as eager about leaving her as she was about being betrothed to Fritz. When he wouldn't move, she conceded slightly.

"Fine. I'll move with you, so you can protect me and save the tree at the same time."

Her words convinced him. As he darted to the left, she moved with him, letting him stay between her and the trolls with every step.

At the edge of the valley, the pixies started screaming and shouting at the trolls. But with their weakened bodies, they sounded no more intimidating than a light wind rustling a few leaves.

A troll swiped an enormous arm at Revyn, attempting to get past him to crush Clara. Revyn jumped and slammed both his feet just above the troll's ankle. The troll stumbled backward while Revyn flipped in the air until he landed safely on two feet again.

He then took Clara's hand and dragged her toward the next tree branch.

As she ran, she noticed Fritz had gone back to working on the crown. On the other side of the valley, King Pavel and his three soldiers stood casually. They watched the fight as if it were an interesting play put on by actors. Since the king only cared about Revyn and about getting a crown made of items from Crystalfall, it made sense that he stayed back. Still, it seemed supremely out of place for them to be standing there when her life was at risk.

Revyn lifted a tree branch and reached for her hand. Before he could grab it, one of the trolls had somehow come up behind her and snatched her around the waist. Its fist squeezed tightly around her middle, pushing out the breath she had in her lungs.

When Revyn tried to come toward her, she screamed at him. "Just save the tree. You can worry about me after that."

Her face must have blazed with conviction because he actually listened to her this time. Except then she realized something she probably should have realized from the start.

While one of the trolls squeezed her, probably hoping to cause her death, two of the other trolls rushed for the tree. With their huge rocky arms, they ripped off golden branches that had only recently been reattached.

Somehow, she had forgotten these trolls destroyed the tree in the first place. It wasn't enough to save the tree. Thanks to Fritz's suggestion, the trolls would now do everything in their power to rip apart the tree—and her—and keep them both from ever being saved.

Her gut sank as the truth settled in. It wasn't enough to distract the trolls and keep them busy until the tree was repaired. To truly save the tree, they had to get rid of the trolls. Even as the troll holding her squeezed and shouted in her ear, she just sighed.

They had to kill the trolls.

Once again, Clara faced an impossible enemy, and she didn't even have a weapon. Then again, instead of focusing on a weapon, her first concern probably needed to be getting out of the grasp of the troll that was currently trying to squeeze her to death.

Her focus turned to the troll's arms and then to her stomach. Nothing there offered a way out. Turning backward, she glanced at the troll's face. It snarled at her and tightened its grip at the same time.

She let out a gasp, losing the last of her air. Her chest heaved, aching to breathe. Even her fingers had difficulty moving when her entire body strained. But it didn't matter now. She had finally seen her way out.

At the same time, she jammed her foot against the troll's elbow and then rammed her own elbow into the troll's stony stomach. If she'd done either action on its own, it probably wouldn't have accomplished much. But done at the same time, her actions served to tilt the troll's arms at the perfect angle so she could slip out from its grip.

Before the troll realized what had happened, her golden slippers had hit the ground. She broke into a run.

A relieved breath escaped from Revyn when he saw her escape the troll's grasp. When he tried to come after her, she just shoved her pointer finger toward Lifespark Tree. "I can take care of the trolls, but I can't save the tree. I need you to focus on that."

He grimaced when another troll lumbered toward her but did as she asked. It would be even harder for him now since several other trolls had ripped off branches, undoing his work while he tried to attach the last few branches.

Clara's chest constricted as she ran. She hadn't caught her breath yet, but she had no time to waste. She had to get to the pixies.

They were slumped on the rocks and soil like before. Their clothes made of gems looked more like clothes made of dull gray rocks. Clara swallowed hard. "I need your help."

Plumia managed to lift her head, but her expression made it clear that whether help was needed or not, it didn't matter. The pixies would not be able to do anything.

Still, Clara had to try. She rolled her shoulders back. "We have to kill the trolls in order to stop them, but I can't do that without a weapon. You gave me this dress and shoes. Can't you make me a weapon too?"

On the very last word of her sentence, a troll reached her and slammed her to the ground. The troll tried to press its heavy foot against her chest, but she managed to roll away just in time. She only allowed herself a single breath before she jumped up and formed a fist with one hand.

It was probably useless, but that wouldn't stop her from trying. Using every ounce of energy inside her, she slammed her fist into the soft skin just under the trolls' arm.

A huge puff of air erupted from the troll's mouth at the contact. It smelled of dead fish and sour olives. The troll stumbled back. But Clara couldn't appreciate the victory at all. It wouldn't be enough. If she'd had a weapon, it would have been enough, but a single punch from a mere mortal?

Already, the troll came at her again, even angrier than before.

Using her smaller size to her advantage, she rushed ahead in one direction, then immediately pivoted to another direction. The troll tried to pursue her. Its large body easily became disoriented when it tried to follow her movements. But even that wasn't enough. The troll was huge, plus two more were coming. They'd get her soon enough.

She managed to glance at the tree. Revyn had done his best, and the trolls mostly ignored him while he worked, but the trolls had also ripped apart branches. There were now over a dozen left to attach, even though a few minutes ago, there had been less than a dozen.

A tight knot formed around Clara's heart. King Pavel and his soldiers continued to watch the spectacle with only the lightest amount of interest. At the top of the hill, Fritz had almost finished with the crown.

In that moment, she finally realized what she'd been trying to ignore. They were going to lose. There were too many trolls and no one left to fight them. If Clara had a weapon, maybe they'd have a slight chance, but the pixies had already lost too much power to help her with that.

Her chin quivered as she ducked to miss a troll's fist. What good had it really done to leave her home? If she had stayed, she would have married Fritz and never been happy again, but wouldn't that have been better than dying?

Inside her chest, the smallest, tiniest spark of warmth lit. It spread outward in tendrils that felt like a roaring fire capable of melting an entire snowstorm. Maybe she was about to die. Maybe she wouldn't get a chance to live as long as she hoped.

But coming to Faerie had given her something she never had in the mortal realm. It gave her a chance to see herself as someone great, as someone who could be impressive, even if she couldn't read.

The spark in her chest grew until it surged through all her limbs. She had power now that she'd never had in the mortal realm. Power no one could take away.

When a troll grabbed her by the ankles and slammed her body against the ground, she just laughed. "You're going to have to do better than that, if you want to stop *me*."

The troll flashed its teeth at her, but she just did the same back at it. The troll growled in response. It growled and then it did something she hadn't expected at all.

It turned away from her.

The troll attacking her and the one next to it, both rushed away from her and headed toward the pixies. The trolls pounded their fists against their palms and ground their teeth with each step.

She gulped and ran after them. The fire in her chest gave her strength, but she knew it might not be enough. Using her agility and small size against them, she managed to reach the pixies first. She struck her limbs outward, trying to turn her body into a wall between the pixies and the trolls.

The trolls took the bait. Their focus immediately shifted away from the pixies. In a flash, they hit Clara with their fists and pinned her to the ground. One of the trolls pressed its foot against her chest, squeezing away the little air she had. The other troll held her feet down, preventing her from kicking her way out of the situation.

Her hands punched, and her hips wriggled, but it didn't matter. She couldn't free herself. The trolls growled above her, and only one thought filled her mind. One thought that frightened and calmed her all at the same time.

At least I got to live one great adventure before I die.

19

Clara struggled to breathe under the weight of the troll's foot. When her life flashed before her eyes, it mostly skipped over her time in the mortal realm. A few nice memories with Heidi surfaced, but the rest blew past in the blink of an eye. Most of her time in the mortal realm had been pointless anyway. And heart breaking and boring and everything she'd wanted to escape when she left.

Now her days in Faerie filled her mind. The rolling hills of Crystalfall with its golden trees, emerald leaves, and glittering jeweled pink flowers. The pixies and their fanciful dances had made her as beautiful as one of the high fae. Even meeting High Queen Winola had been illuminating and grand.

The memories swirled inside her, giving her peace in these last few moments. They sparked and twinkled so strongly in her mind that she didn't realize when the sparking started happening outside her body too.

Narrowing her eyes, she managed to glance to the side. Near her right arm, lightning began to strike. The lightning strikes glowed golden with a touch of pink. As soon as one struck the ground, another one appeared to replace it. By the third strike, she realized the lightning was moving closer to her hand.

Instead of pulling away from it like she might have done in the mortal realm, something in her heart told her to do the opposite, so she stretched her fingers out until the next lightning bolt struck in the center of her palm.

It didn't hurt. It didn't zing or shake. It sent a tingling energy into her palm that quickly spread into her fingers as well. Keeping her hand in place, she waited for the next lightning strike. When that one hit, it didn't just tingle against her skin.

It started forming an object. A new lightning strike hit and then a new one. Her lips tilted upward as the item took shape. A sword.

The magical weapon had a golden hilt with pink gems embedded in the cross guard. The silvery blade gleamed gold as the last lightning strike hit. Energy tingled inside her as she lifted her gaze to the source of the lightning.

Plumia flew with her hands out in front of her. The color had completely drained from her face, which still had twice the determination Clara had ever seen. Though it felt like several long minutes, the entire weapon had only taken a second or two to form.

The moment it was finished, Plumia dropped from the air into a heap on the black soil. The other pixies lifted their arms, but all of them were too weak to rush to Plumia's side.

This weapon had been created through great sacrifice, and Clara would not waste it. Gripping the sword tight in her hand, she immediately shoved it into the soft spot under the nearest troll's arm.

Ice cold blood gushed from the wound. She had to spin to the side just to avoid the falling troll. The troll holding her feet pulled its hands back, ready to punch her. The moment it lifted its arms, she sliced her new weapon into that troll's armpit. It fell to the ground immediately.

Now she whirled the sword around in a circle and ran toward the nearest troll. She'd never trained with any weapon in her life. Since she'd just managed to kill two trolls in two blows, she either had incredible prodigy-like skills, or—more likely—the weapon had been imbued with some sort of pixie magic to give her skills she never would have had on her own.

When she reached her third troll, she killed that one, too, giving more weight to the magic weapon theory. Only three trolls remained.

One of them studiously ripped branches from the tree. Somehow, Revyn had continued working so hard that there were still only about a dozen branches to reattach, even after all the ones the trolls had broken off.

But he wasn't reattaching any tree branches now. He wasn't even looking at the trolls.

He just stood with his arms at his side and his mouth open wide, staring straight at Clara. Yes, she decided, impressing him was officially her favorite activity. His gaze jumped to her sword and then to her face and then to the trolls and then to her face again.

A little smile tugged at the corners of his lips. For a moment, she wondered if he'd keep on standing there just so he could have a perfect view as she fought the rest of the trolls.

She whirled her weapon around with a little more flourish than necessary. At that, his mouth turned to a wide grin. He winked at her, and then grabbed the nearest tree branch. After tossing it into the air, he caught it and melded it against the tree trunk in a single breath. Apparently, he wanted to impress her too.

It worked.

But the trolls had finally decided killing Clara was the only thing that mattered. One of them rushed toward her. It held its arms tight against its body and slammed into her with the full force of its chest. This would be trickier since it covered the weak part of its body with its stone-like arms.

Testing out her magic weapon, she tried piercing its neck. The blade bounced off without even scratching the troll's skin.

No matter. She had another idea. Twirling to one side, she jabbed the sword toward the troll's arm, as if intending to force the blade between the arm and the troll's body. The arm protected its weak spot, but the troll still had enough fear to use its opposite hand to protect the spot even more.

But she hadn't been aiming for that spot. Not really. Instead, she had expected the troll to protect its soft spot, and she had already calculated just how much its other arm would move by doing so.

Once the opposite arm went to protect the weak spot, she immediately changed her sword's direction until it landed deep within the troll's weak spot on the other side. A moment later, the troll landed against the black soil with a heavy thud.

The last two trolls panted and growled at her, but they didn't charge. They had finally stopped trying to destroy the tree. Though she knew killing the trolls was the only way before, she also could see things had shifted now.

She moved closer to the tree while Revyn worked on attaching the last few branches. "Revyn, are trolls bound by bargains the same way the high fae are?"

Revyn nodded as he attached a branch to the tree. "All creatures are bound if they make a bargain, even mortals. If a bargain is made, Faerie itself will force the creature to fulfill that bargain."

Turning back to the trolls, Clara lifted one eyebrow. "Let's make a bargain. I will let you leave this valley with your lives."

The trolls started backing away.

She immediately took a step forward, pointing her sword at the nearest troll's armpit. "In return, you will *never* return to Crystalfall for any reason. And you'll free the mermaid you have captured in your cavern." She let the words settle, and then to be extra certain, she added a few more. "You will never return to Crystalfall for the rest of your lives."

The trolls glanced at each other. One of them halfheartedly curled its hand into a fist. But when it lifted its arm to aim, she set the tip of her sword against the soft spot under the troll's arm.

After a gurgling gasp, the troll backed away. The other troll hit itself in the chest. "Accept." The troll nodded. "Accept."

Taking a step forward, Clara glared at the second troll. "And you?"

With a heavy sigh, the second troll nodded too. "Accept."

"Good." She lowered her sword to her side. "Then leave. I never want to see another troll ever again."

The trolls opened a Faerie door and disappeared through it right away.

Revyn raised an eyebrow at her as soon as they were gone. "There are other trolls in Fairfrost. Many other trolls."

Her gut clenched. "Do you think the other trolls will come here and destroy this tree?"

"No." Revyn shook his head. "Trolls live in packs, and they do not care at all about the other packs. This pack was the only one that wanted to destroy the pixie's tree. The others do not care. I just find it curious that you spared their lives and even thought to rescue that mermaid. I do not know of any fae who would have done the same."

She shrugged in response. "I didn't want to lose my own life. I figured they would feel the same."

Biting her lip, she glanced back at the pixies. All of them looked as sickly and weak as before. Plumia's body appeared especially dull. Clara's gaze turned back to the tree.

Only six branches still needed to be attached. The moment Revyn followed her gaze, he immediately lifted branches and melded them against the trunk. It must have gotten easier for him after practicing with the others. He attached the final tree branches with ease.

The moment he added the last one, a huge pulsing glow lit at the center of the trunk and then spread out throughout the rest of the trunk and branches. For several seconds, the tree glowed so brightly that it lit the area around them as if it were midday.

Another huge pulse lit the tree even more, and the sound of jingling bells started. They chimed quietly at first, but the sound grew in volume until it filled the entire valley.

Eventually, the glowing of the tree faded little by little. The sound of the bells lessened too. In another few moments, the tree stood as golden and shiny as all the other trees in Crystalfall, but it no longer glowed.

When Clara glanced back at the pixies, they had not risen from their spots on the rocks and the soil, but the jewels on their clothing had the same sparkle and brightness as when she'd first met them. Each of the pixies rubbed their heads. It would probably take some time before they felt completely back to normal again, but clearly, it was happening.

A smile lifted Clara's lips. She was overcome with the urge to shout for joy, to twirl around, and to throw herself into Revyn's arms all at the same time.

Before she could do any of those things, she was abruptly reminded that she, Revyn, and the pixies were not the only ones there.

"It's finished." Fritz stood at the top of the hill with a crown of green pearls sitting on the palm of his hand.

Clara swallowed hard. Tingling shivered through her limbs, turning her whole body rigid and tense. How had she forgotten about the crown?

He started down the hill with his head held high as he looked over at the Fairfrost king. "Don't forget that you made your own bargain with me. I got you your stupid Crystalfall crown, which you easily could have made for yourself if you had only tried. Now, you are required to take me to the creation magic."

King Pavel held out one hand expectantly. His three guards stood behind him, still wearing expressions of indifference.

Fritz dropped a calculating stare on each of them, but then he tossed the crown into the air, throwing it to the Fairfrost king.

The tightness in Clara's gut turned from anxious to determined. The high queen of Faerie had said only Faerie itself could choose the leaders for Crystalfall. Maybe King Pavel was willing to defy Faerie, but she wasn't.

Gritting her teeth, she swiped her sword through the air. In a single slice, Fritz's crudely-made crown shattered into tiny pieces. The broken pearl strands dropped to the ground as heavily as her cup and saucer had back at her parents' annual Christmas party.

Fritz hissed through his teeth and formed fists with his hands. He lifted them and started toward Clara with murder in his eyes.

Revyn took a single step forward and grabbed a handful of Fritz's collar. Holding the clothing, Revyn lifted Fritz off the ground. Then Revyn spoke in a voice that could only be described as a growl. "You will leave her alone or else you will die."

The moment Revyn touched the collar, Fritz started squirming and gulping and trying to wriggle free. Revyn set him down, and Fritz immediately took several steps back. He had been set on edge more than usual, and clearly, had difficultly calming himself down.

After one last hard swallow, he turned away from Revyn. Despite the change in position, Fritz's knocking knees were obvious. However, he still did his best to ignore Revyn, turning to the king. "You still have to show me where the creation magic is. I never actually said I would get you a crown, I just said I knew how to get it. And I did. Now you have to fulfill your part of the bargain."

King Pavel let out a hardened chuckle. "*We* never made a bargain. You just made a claim and then a request, but unlike the trolls, I am bound by nothing."

He dismissed Fritz with a wave of his hand. Now he turned to Revyn. "This mortal girl told me all about how the pixies enchanted you."

Revyn's eyebrow rose as he turned to Clara.

The king continued before anyone else had a chance to speak. "Since you are clearly more simple-minded than I realized, you may no longer guard the castle. When you return to Fairfrost, I want you to go to the outer city of Balalov instead."

The confusion on Revyn's face at the mention of the enchantment immediately vanished at the mention of his new assignment. Now a light sparked in his stormy eyes that lifted the heaviness weighing down his features. For the first time since Clara had met him, he wore true happiness. True relief.

In a flash, the look was wiped away. He replaced it with one of mock sadness. "Of course, my king. I understand."

Even though he attempted a sad tone, Clara could still hear joy in his words. She had been right then. Being sent to an outer city would make it much easier for Revyn and his brother to escape Fairfrost.

Without another word, King Pavel opened a door, and he and his three soldiers disappeared through it. Revyn might never have to see the king again.

The moment they went out of sight, Fritz let out a scream that shook the air. "Why is everyone so stupid? No one appreciates my genius. Or my ambition."

He jerked his head toward Clara. An untamed look danced in his eyes. One of his eyes twitched repeatedly as he bared his teeth. "I'll find the creation magic myself then. I prefer doing things myself anyway because then they actually get done."

As he started climbing the hill, he kept muttering to himself, his tone growing more unhinged with each step. "Just you wait. I *will* find that creation magic, and I will take the magic inside myself so that I too can have power like the fae. I will become the most powerful being in all of Faerie." He started a crazed chuckling that shook in the air. "I'll take over everything. I will take over this entire court."

Clara leaned a little closer to Revyn and took in a steady breath. Only then was she ready to speak again. "You will not take over. You'll be stopped."

Fritz had reached the top of the hill now. He whirled around with eyes wide and his mouth in a twisted smile. "I will destroy anyone who stands in my way. Who could be strong enough to stop me?"

Revyn reached an arm around Clara's waist as he stood tall. "The entire court will stand in your way."

Fritz's eyes narrowed. "Then I will destroy the entire court. I'll destroy Crystalfall." He gave that same crazed laugh again, which sent goose bumps across Clara's arms.

Then he looked down at them with his lip curling. "Believe me when I say *nothing* will stop me."

He didn't wait around for more arguments after that. He stomped off, erupting in wild laughter every few steps.

When he had gone far enough away that his laughter couldn't be heard anymore, Clara dared to look into Revyn's eyes. He pulled her a little closer when she did.

"The pixies are starting to get up. They'll be heading to the nearest revel now."

She leaned closer to him and looked up at him through her eyelashes. "Don't you have to get back to Fairfrost to save your brother?"

"Yes." He flashed a roguish grin. "But I can do that in the morning. After a victory like this, it is only fitting that we revel."

She matched his grin with one of her own. Her heart skipped in her chest.

Whirling her around, he tucked her arm into the crook of his. "And this time, you will be dancing with me."

20

TWINKLING LIGHTS AND UPBEAT MUSIC filled the thicket Clara and Revyn stepped into. She went straight for one of the tables and lifted a golden plate. Without a second thought, she said "Asparagus with hollandaise sauce and potatoes." The food appeared on the plate instantly, and when she took a bite, it tasted better than any asparagus and potatoes she had ever eaten in the mortal realm.

When Revyn glanced at it, she handed him her fork, allowing him to have a taste. He chewed and swallowed, and even nodded after he had finished. But he wasn't done yet.

With a challenge in his eye, Revyn grabbed his own plate, and said, "Solyanka." A steaming bowl with a salty and sour broth sat on the plate in front of him. Chunks of meat and diced vegetables floated around, giving off the scent of herbs. He nudged it toward her.

Reaching for the spoon that had appeared, she tried her first bite of Faerie food. Her entire body melted, and a little moan escaped her mouth once the soup hit her tongue. She had never tasted anything so exquisite in her life. Revyn thrust his chest out and grinned.

It was a good thing she had no intention of ever returning to the mortal realm again. If she did, the food there would surely taste like dust compared to the delicious Faerie food before her.

He allowed her a few more spoonfuls of the soup, but then his face turned eager as he tugged her to the middle of the thicket for a dance.

They didn't dance any of the dances she knew in the mortal realm, but it didn't matter. His arms were sure around her. He led her with perfect ease in graceful twirls and jumps. The music was lively, probably putting red into her cheeks.

But the more she danced, the more she wanted to continue. Her feet didn't hurt this time, and she was no longer exhausted. She just wanted to continue dancing because being with Revyn made her feel alive in a way she never wanted to forget. Couldn't forget. For the first time, she felt like she was truly living instead of just existing.

When a slower, more romantic melody began, their dance changed to one that matched. Soon, he held her only inches away. Their bodies swayed and stepped, but they still had ample opportunity to stare into each other's eyes.

It should have been easy to keep her gaze on his, especially since his stormy eyes had the most beautiful specks of blue in them. But somehow, her gaze kept trailing downward to his lips.

Each time it did, he pulled her just a little bit closer.

Soon, they were nearly nose to nose. He smiled before speaking. "Most fae do not care for anyone except themselves. You saw how King Pavel acted during the fight. That is how nearly all fae are. They act only out of their own self-interest."

Considering how the king and his soldiers had paid only the slightest attention while the trolls nearly killed Clara, she could see what he meant.

Revyn continued. "But I care for my brother. I thought if I started to care for someone new…" He dropped his head lower until the tip of his nose touched hers. "I thought I would not be able to care for my brother anymore."

After their noses touched, her entire body was aflutter and she could barely think let alone speak. Heat climbed up her neck. She only managed a single word in response. "And?"

Revyn stopped dancing then. "I do care for him still. I care for him as much as I always have, but…"

He stood in silence for several seconds as he stared to the side. Words seemed to be as elusive for him as they had been for her. When he finally looked at her again, his gaze lured her in like bait.

His hand reached up, tucking a strand of hair behind her ear. "I do not understand how, but you have captured my heart. I suddenly cannot imagine a future unless you are in it."

The last bit of sense that she had left evaporated away with those words. She leaned into him with all the longing her years in a suffocating betrothal had not allowed.

When she lifted herself up on her tiptoes, he came down to meet her at the same time. His lips that pressed against hers were hot and soft and just as magical as the revel around them.

He wrapped his arms tighter around her waist, pulling her even closer as the kiss deepened. Her hand started at his shoulder—where it had been sitting for the dance—but now it trailed higher until her fingers tangled into the inviting strands of his silky hair.

She felt the kiss everywhere inside her, but mostly in her heart. He held her gently, brushing his hand across her back.

When he pulled away to look into her eyes again, her pulse could not stop dancing. With the smallest grin on his lips, he leaned in again for a kiss even more ravenous than the first.

The world could have been burning around them, and Clara never would have known. So entranced she was by her nutcracker of Crystalfall.

It probably would have lasted longer except for the familiar sound of twinkling bells nearby. They pulled away, but Revyn kept his arms around her. She turned toward the noise, resting her cheek against his chest.

Plumia flew next to them wearing the face of a creature who had known death a little too closely. Several pixies surrounded her. Their skin practically glowed and their jeweled clothes sparkled and glittered. Plumia looked even more alive than ever.

The moment was perfect. Well, almost perfect.

Right then, Clara remembered the terrible truth she immediately wanted to shove away and forget forever. The fae were immortal. Revyn would live forever, while Clara would age and die just like mortals always did.

Something about Plumia's face reminded her of that. Even though the pixie smiled, she looked a little sad at seeing Clara wrapped in Revyn's arms.

But even if the pixie was remembering Clara's mortality, it did not stop her from lifting both her arms into the air and speaking loudly. "You saved us, Clara of the mortal realm. You saved Lifespark Tree even though you had no bargain, vow, or favor that required you to do so. During the fight with the trolls, you even stood like a shield in front of us and stopped the trolls from hurting us when we were our most vulnerable."

The pixies around her nodded and fluttered their wings, giving off delightful chimes.

Now Plumia's face turned more serious. "I once learned from a wise young mortal that sometimes actions do not have to be compelled by bargains, vows, favors, or even personal interest. Sometimes, actions can be compelled by honor."

At the sound of that word, Clara immediately remembered the conversation she'd had with the pixie about honor.

Plumia raised her hand and glanced back at the other pixies. When she did, they all nodded, and a new song started. Plucked cello strings created a bouncing base theme. Only a moment later, bells with a celestial tinkling sound joined in. The song had a playful melody as beautiful as Plumia herself.

Flying and swooping in time with the music, the pixies danced around Clara. As they moved, a golden necklace with a large pink diamond pendant began forming around her neck. The pink jewel sparkled in the twinkling light of the thicket.

She could feel the energy that buzzed inside it down to her very bones. It filled her body with a sensation of life.

When the pixies finished and flew back behind Plumia, that sad look in her eye had disappeared. An expression of pure joy replaced it now.

"I do not have the magic to make you truly immortal, but this amulet will greatly slow your aging." Plumia flew a little higher and gestured toward the golden necklace. "Someday you will die of old age, but with this amulet, you will live many ages longer than you would have without it."

The pixie glanced at Revyn and back to Clara. She threw them both a smirk. "I am certain you will find a use for such magic."

Clara touched the amulet, hardly able to breathe. Was it possible her life could have turned from such misery to such perfection in such a short time? She knew it couldn't possibly be a dream, and yet, she still had difficulty believing it was real.

Reality was easier to accept when Revyn pulled her a little closer again. He brushed two fingers across the pink diamond pendant and smiled.

She knew better than to say *thank you*, but she still nodded at the pixies and placed her hands over her chest with an expression that hopefully said it for her. When they flew away, their chiming wings sounded happier than ever.

Turning back to Revyn, she caught him looking off into the distance.

After several moments of silence, Clara whispered to him. "Are you thinking about your brother?"

"Yes." Revyn immediately reached for the blue knit scarf around his neck. He touched it like it was the key to his brother's rescue.

"I think we've reveled enough," she said. "Let's go find your brother and bring him back to Crystalfall."

The smile that split across Revyn's face sent Clara into a fit of flutters once again. His eyes looked brighter than ever. "I cannot wait for you to meet him. Ludo can be a bit grumpy in some circumstances, but in the most endearing way. He has always been a good brother to me."

Clara took Revyn's hand and started leading him away from the thicket. She had a feeling Revyn had always been a good brother too. She gestured at the empty space ahead. "Let's go then. Let's go meet Ludo."

Revyn opened his Faerie door, which smelled of peppermint and pomegranate and had walls of sparkling blue smoke. Whatever adventure awaited them next, Clara was excited they'd be facing it together.

THE STORY CONTINUES

Are you dying to know the **ruler and fate of Crystalfall**? Find out in the Fae and Crystal Thorns series!

Join a new main character, Chloe, and her fae warrior, Quintus. Start with Book 1, *Flame & Crystal Thorns*.

She's a human apothecary. He's the fae warrior who once broke her heart… and now he needs her help.

Flame & Crystal Thorns is available now!

AUTHOR'S NOTE

NOVEMBER IS NOT my favorite time of year. Without delving too much into the details, my kind and loving parents were killed in a car accident when I was only 12 years old. As you may have guessed, the accident happened in November—the day before Thanksgiving, in fact.

It hits me every year, but this year (2022) was a little different. This year, I am the exact same age my mom was when she died. For most of the year, I did my best to not think about it. I told myself it's just an age, and it doesn't mean anything.

But then November hit.

It's pretty weird being the age my mom was when she died. It's weird that I'm now older than she ever was. It's surreal, painful, and honestly, kind of scary. If I ever needed a distraction, I needed it this November.

That's how this story was born. I wrote this story to distract myself but also to remind myself that even the scariest, most intense circumstances can still be worked through. No matter what happens in life, eventually, a happy "ending" can be found.

This story was for me, but most of all, this story is for you. In searching out and creating my own joy, I desperately wanted to share that joy with others.

I hope you'll consider this story a gift from me to you for whatever holiday/birthday you happen to be celebrating next. I hope this book uplifts you and reminds you happiness can be found even after the most troubling circumstances. I hope this story is a reminder that you have greatness inside you.

Happy holidays and happy reading!
Kay L. Moody

ABOUT THE AUTHOR

Kay L. Moody is proud to be an epic fantasy romance author who gets to create worlds for a living. ;) Her books feature strong female characters, court intrigue, royalty, magic, and slow burn romance with men who fall first.

With 17 romantasy books across 4 complete series, she's no stranger to hidden princesses, deadly competitions, or couples who go from enemies to lovers. Her books have sold more than 100,000 copies worldwide and have earned accolades including *Best Fantasy Book* (Many Books, Dec 2023) and *Bestseller: Fantasy* (BookRaid, Apr 2024).

Her favorite non bookish things are pizza, summertime, the color pink, and having pretty nails. She lives in the western USA with her husband and four sons. Follow her on social media to stay in touch (@kaylmoody).

ALSO BY KAY L. MOODY

Fae and Crystal Thorns

Flame & Crystal Thorns
Shadow & Crystal Thorns
Blade & Crystal Thorns
Curse & Crystal Thorns
Wrath & Crystal Thorns
Standalone: Nutcracker of Crystalfall

The Fae of Bitter Thorn

Heir of Bitter Thorn
Court of Bitter Thorn
Castle of Bitter Thorn
Crown of Bitter Thorn
Queen of Bitter Thorn

The Elements of Kamdaria

The Elements of the Crown
The Elements of the Gate
The Elements of the Storm

Truth Seer Trilogy

Truth Seer
Healer
Truth Changer

Visit **kaylmoody.com/beauty** to download a bonus
story, *Bargain of Power and Beauty*, for free.

BONUS STORY
BARGAIN OF POWER AND BEAUTY

Visit **kaylmoody.com/beauty** to download your copy

To receive special offers, bonus content, and info on new releases, sign up for Kay L. Moody's email list! You'll also get this story for FREE. *Bargain of Power and Beauty* is a romantic standalone story from Fae and Crystal Thorns.
Power is dangerous. Beauty is fatal.
Love is the only risk worth taking.

MORE FROM KAY L. MOODY

Don't Miss This Related Series!

Swords first, love later. That was always her rule.

Elora lives for her sword, but her skill can't save her family from ruin. To protect them, she accepts an arranged marriage, only to be stolen away by a broodingly handsome fae prince before she can say "I do." Now trapped in his cursed court by a magical bargain, she must train him to win a throne, but the greatest battle she faces might be the one for her own heart.

Book 1:
COURT OF BITTER THORN

MORE FROM KAY L. MOODY

You Also Might Like Kay L. Moody's Previous Series!

She's not the only one who will do anything to win…

A girl from the slums with a rare and powerful magic must win a cutthroat competition to save her family. But her greatest rival, a privileged, arrogant, and annoyingly handsome prodigy, is the one person who could expose all her secrets and ruin everything.

Book 1:
THE ELEMENTS OF THE CROWN